CHRISTMAS CONFESSIONS

BOOK TWO OF THE MISSED CONNECTIONS TRILOGY

KATHRYN REIGN

Christmas Confessions

Book Two of the Missed Connections Trilogy

© Copyright 2022 Kathryn Reign

Cover Design by Covers by Combs

CONTENTS

CHRISTMAS CONFESSIONS

BOOK TWO OF THE MISSED CONNECTIONS TRILOGY

KATHRYN REIGN

1

———

GISELLE

I'm a pretty freaking hot A-list celebrity. Especially tonight. This blood-red Versace gown was basically made to be on *my* thin, supermodel body exclusively. And by the way everyone here is staring at me, I know they all agree.

I'm at a charity gala event thing with Eliza—one of my best friends, despite the age difference, whom I'm trying desperately to forget I shared a romantic kiss with not long ago—and her husband, who is sick with ALS,

Shawn. I don't even really know what I'm doing here, but I accepted Eliza and Shawn's invite ages ago and don't want to be one of those people who cancels on them last minute.

Eliza and I haven't really talked much since our accidental kiss in the stairwell at her office. When it happened, after we broke apart, Eliza's pale blue eyes widened as she gasped, then she told me it had been a huge mistake, and that it would never happen again. I don't know if she's the one who never wants it to happen again, or if she just thinks it's what *I* want, but I definitely don't want that.

I have a massive crush on Eliza. I always have, pretty much since the night I met her. With her long and silvery blonde hair, her petite frame, and her incredible style, how could I not?

I don't know if I always found myself more attracted to women than to men, but I came to accept who I was, fully, when I was twenty. It was at that age that I stopped dating boys and stopped lying to myself—I'm just not into them.

Unfortunately, I'm not ready to come out of the closet to my family, friends, or fans yet, so I haven't exactly ever gotten the chance to date a girl—or woman—either. I've been single for well over five years, and I'm sort of sick of it.

At first, when I met Eliza, I didn't think she could ever possibly feel the same way about me, especially considering the fact that she's been married to Shawn for practically *forever.* But I *had* been wondering these past couple of weeks if maybe I was wrong. If maybe she did like me. I always caught her staring at me, for one. And two, she was always constantly finding reasons to bring me around. She invited me to events like this one, to parties at her house, to photoshoots at her office, to Thanksgiving—I mean, *come on!* Freaking *Thanksgiving!*

Since the kiss happened, now I know for certain that she feels something for me in return. It makes what she said right after the kiss even harder to deal with.

There are a lot of celebrities here tonight. Taking pictures outside had been exhausting. I much prefer structured photoshoots and runway events over standing in front of a bunch of cameras with people all screaming at me at the same time, Bryan and Lonnie—my bodyguards—having to hang close with my every move.

"Well, I know *I* definitely need a drink after all that," Eliza huffs once we've taken our seats at a small lounge area next to some C-list TV show stars inside this insanely extravagant event hall.

Almost instantly, a waiter appears to take our drink order and hands us complimentary glasses of champagne while we wait.

Shawn, in his nice Hugo Boss suit with his expensive hand-carved walking cane, carefully crosses one of his weak, slow-moving legs over the other. "I don't know how many times I heard them asking you who you were here with tonight," he comments, looking directly at me. I feel myself blushing as I avoid Eliza's eyes.

"Oh, I *know*," I reply. "They're so nosy, aren't they? Clearly, I came out of the same limo as you two."

"I read that some people think you're my adopted daughter," Shawn says with a chuckle.

It could look that way. With his scruffy long beard and graying dark hair, he's looking almost like a stylish grandpa tonight. But really, he's only in his fifties. I think it's the beard and his ALS that makes him look older.

I smirk at him. "*I* read that I'm actually a lovechild of yours, and that the woman who birthed me passed away, so I came to LA *just* to meet you." I'd seen it on a blog post that one of my friends sent to me on Instagram. It had actually made me laugh out loud.

The thought of people thinking I am some sort of stepdaughter to Eliza sort of weirds me out, though.

"Just curious, though," Shawn says. I have to lean in a little to hear him. He speaks slowly because of the ALS, but it's also just so loud in here with everyone talking and the loud pop music blaring. "Why didn't you bring someone? I said you could."

I bite my bottom lip. This time, I can't help it—I want to sneak a peek at Eliza. When I do, I find that she's suddenly found the glittery sheer curtains behind our sofa incredibly fascinating. She's acting as if she isn't even hearing us.

"Um, I don't know," I tell him honestly.

"Are you seeing anyone?" he asks. "Have you ever *had* a boyfriend? I don't think I ever even hear you talk about boys."

"Why would I bore you with that?" I ask, my stomach dipping.

Shawn rolls his eyes. "I have to endure a lot more

boring conversations, I promise you that. You should hear these doctors at the appointments I go to."

My stomach sinks some more. I hate the idea of Shawn going to doctors' appointments at all, because it only reminds me that his ALS is quickly getting worse and how stressed out and sad Eliza is over it. I hate that she's hurting inside.

But I also hate that she doesn't want to kiss me again.

I laugh at Shawn's joke, even though I don't think it's funny. "Fine," I say to him. "If you *must* know, I *do* have a boyfriend. We just haven't decided if we want to go public yet or not."

Eliza's eyes fly to mine, but when she sees that I was looking right at her when I said it, she chokes on something invisible and gets to her feet. "Sorry, goodness me!" she cries, patting her chest.

"You don't say!" Shawn gasps, clearly excited for me.

I beam at him and ignore Eliza in her stupid, beautiful, silver Coco Chanel gown as she scans the room as if she's in search of better people to converse with. I hope she's hearing my every word. And I hope she's jealous.

"Yeah, he's super great," I continue.

"Who is it?" Shawn asks, side-glancing at his pretending-not-to-hear-me-wife.

I shake my head and wiggle a finger at him. "Nuh uh. Not saying. Not *now*, anyway. And especially not *here*." I turn and stare at the C-listers whom I can tell are hanging onto my every word.

"Eliza, sit down, will you?" Shawn calls to his wife.

She does as she's told, now done with her coughing fit. "Sorry, I was just hoping the waiter would come back so I could ask him for some water. What did I miss?"

"Liza, Giselle here has landed herself a boyfriend!"

Eliza gives me a pleasant smile. It doesn't reach her beautiful, mesmerizing, soul-trapping eyes. I try my best to give her a private look that says, *I wish I was with you, but you don't want me, and I'm sad.* If she notices it, she doesn't say so.

"Well, I'm very happy for you, Giselle," she tells me, giving my leg a gentle squeeze, sending goosebumps shooting up my spine, nearly making me flinch. How can she touch me like that right in front of Shawn?!

"Thank you, Eliza," I say in a formal tone. "Grab my drink for me when it comes, will you?" I stand up and smooth out my dress.

"Where are you going?" Shawn asks.

"Uh, I have to pee," I lie. I really just want to get away from Eliza before I burst into disappointed tears all over again.

2

BRENNAN

It's been two whole days since the anonymous post came out about my brother, Derek Heed, being some sort of abusive boyfriend. I get why my parents wouldn't be over it yet, but they keep talking about it as if it's the absolute end of the entire world. They didn't even want me to go into work today at the sporting goods store that I own. They told me what Derek was going through should have warranted me taking a few days off.

Derek plays college football. And he's damn good at it. I get that it's risky for the lies to be spread about Derek right now. I get how it could harm the chances of him going to the NFL. But it isn't like he was diagnosed with some incurable disease. It isn't like there are rumors going around that he murdered someone and is on the FBI's most wanted list.

Someone lied—it definitely was a lie—and said he liked to scream, manhandle, and hit his ex-girlfriends. The person who made the post probably wasn't even Derek's actual girlfriend ever. I bet if they got someone to track it, they would find that it was just from some lonely old cook who lived on the opposite side of the country.

I told my parents that I was definitely still going into work today, no matter how dire of a situation my older brother had currently found himself in, but now that I'm back home for the day, they want me to sit in the living room with them so they can keep discussing it.

"Poor Selena," Mom says about Derek's wife, whom I could care less about, dabbing her eyes with a tissue, the TV still playing the news channel. It hadn't been turned off since the post was made, and I am beginning to think if they turn it off now, the little headline scroll at the bottom of the news channel is going to be permanently etched onto the screen.

"Why 'poor Selena?'" I ask. I still haven't ruled out that she's the one who made up the lie. I wouldn't put it past her. To me, she has always seemed like the type of woman who is just into Derek for the fame that he's starting to gain. And the money he already has, which will probably quadruple when he makes it to the NFL.

"Derek told us no one will leave her alone. That she can't even leave her house in fear of people questioning and accusing her."

Huh, so I'm not the only one who thinks so.

"How do you guys know she isn't the one who wrote it?" I ask. I've brought it up before, but they were quick to just change the subject, so I figure, why not give it another try?

My mother looks like I've personally insulted her. "What do you mean? Why would you even ask that?"

I shrug, feeling a little uncomfortable. "I mean, she *is* the one who's with Derek right now. What if she wants the attention?" Am I so wrong for wondering it?

Dad shakes his head at me. His overgrown haircut is starting to look a little like mine, just with gray added, and it makes me feel much older than just twenty-six. Dad didn't age that well, so I am afraid that I won't, either. "Selena is a good girl. She wouldn't do something like that. Besides, the post said that it was somebody from his past. They refer to Derek as their old boyfriend. Not husband."

I know I shouldn't keep arguing, but I can't help it. "Well, yeah… But that doesn't mean that it's not her. If she put wife, since Derek's only had one of those, everyone would know it was her."

"Brennan, knock it off." Mom has had enough of my bullshit.

I sigh.

I just don't know what to think anymore. I don't

know why somebody would do this to Derek. He's my big brother, and we've always looked out for each other. Him more than me, if anything. Maybe that means it's my turn to do the looking out. Maybe I'm supposed to figure out who's behind all of this.

I stand up.

"Where are you going?" Mom asks in an angry tone. Heaven forbid I do anything when Derek is in distress.

"I've got to go talk to someone," I tell them.

"Who?" they ask together.

"Doesn't matter. At least not yet. I'll let you know. Just, stay calm. Don't talk to the press or anyone. We'll get this sorted out."

I head upstairs, hop on my parents' ancient computer, and do some research. The social media kind. I want to find an old friend I went to high school with. I ran into her at a bar not too long ago, and she acted as if she couldn't stand the sight of me.

Leah Olson.

I need to ask her some questions.

3

———

DAMASCUS

*B*lair Cosgrove makes me feel alive.

More alive than I have ever felt since Jennifer—my ex who ripped my heart out and stomped on it while making eye contact with me—anyway.

I would have never expected a double date half-planned by my best friend's girlfriend, Sara, to go as well as it did, and I definitely never expected to like someone who is so completely different from me, but here I am.

Blair is like… a nerd? Not like that stereotypical

movie nerd, but she's super smart and obedient and respectful. She is always mindful of her curfew and wants things done the right way. She's super focused on school and graduating.

But on top of all of that, she still knows how to have fun. She still knows how to bend the rules a little as long as it's not going to really harm anything. Like the fact that she has a fake ID, even though she's about to turn twenty-one soon. She doesn't drink all the time like I do, but she doesn't mind letting loose once in a while, especially after an extra-long day of studying or doing homework.

When I was with Jennifer, a dark-haired vixen with a silky-smooth voice, I would go through phases where I needed a break from her. I only liked to hang out with her maybe a few times a week. The crazy thing with Blair is that I've seen her pretty much every day since that day at the pool hall.

It's been twenty-five days, and I've maybe not seen her for four of them.

And when I'm not with her, it's absolutely ridiculous how much I miss her. Even Andrew and Sara give me crap for it.

"It's your guys' fault!" I had told them. How can they be mad at me for talking about Blair nonstop when Andy's girlfriend is the one who introduced us?

Blair is coming over to my apartment today because, apparently, she's a really good cook, and I have been telling her that she needs to prove it to me, so she said she'd come by and show me her masterful ways. She said we could do it at her house, but that she wasn't thrilled about the idea of her parents being around. She's not moving out until she graduates. While it makes me feel like I'm sort of dating a high schooler, it's kind of cute, too.

It's Sara who answers the door when Blair gets to our apartment.

"Surprise, surprise! Hi, Blair," Sara greets her.

Blair looks surprised to see them. But gorgeous as always. She's in a cute off-shoulder top and leggings. Her strawberry blonde hair is pulled up high into a ponytail, making her bold blue eyes pop out even more than they usually do.

"Oh! I didn't know you and Andy were going to be here! But I brought plenty of food. Do you guys want me to cook dinner for you, too?"

Sara steps aside and lets her in, and when our eyes land on each other, my stomach dips. I've missed this feeling, but I'm terrified of it, too. And even though I have this wonderful, amazing, unique, specimen spending all of her time with me, I still find myself thinking about Jennifer.

I'm not nearly as miserable as I was before Blair, but that doesn't mean it doesn't still hurt. Jennifer ripped my heart out and threw it to the ground. I'm not saying I've fallen for Blair, but maybe the reason I'm holding back from doing so is because I don't want her to do the same.

Andy walks out of the hallway to the bedrooms, having heard what Blair said. "Oh, no, we're out of here," he tells her. "We will let you two have your alone time, or whatever."

Blair looks slightly embarrassed, and it's adorable the way the apples of her cheeks turn pink. It makes me want to go over and kiss them.

When Andy and Sara finally leave us alone, I walk over to Blair and wrap my arms tightly around her. She's so short and petite that I have to physically hunch over to rest my chin on top of her head. I love how small she is compared to me.

She looks up at me, and our lips instantly collide. She has on that grapefruit-flavored ChapStick I love so much. I think she wears it now just for me.

"Mm," I say when I pull away.

She grins at me flirtatiously and goes into the kitchen to start digging through the bag she brought.

"So, what are we having?"

"Well, I remember you telling me last week about how you are obsessed with Sloppy Joes."

"Sloppy Joes? That's your grand gourmet meal idea to prove to me that you're a good cook?" I tease. "I don't know if you know this, but that's not exactly the most difficult thing to make."

I sit on the barstool at the counter and observe her. I love the way she moves around my kitchen as if she lives here. It makes me wish she did.

What the hell is wrong with me? It's only been twenty-five days.

She shoots me a playful glare. "These aren't just *any* Sloppy Joes," she explains. "I am making the seasoning and tomato sauce myself! Not to mention, I have a secret ingredient that will blow your mind, too."

"Blow my mind, huh?" I ask, raising my eyebrows. "That's a pretty bold statement to assume."

But she looks fairly confident. She gets to work and starts cooking, and I would've thought I would get bored sitting here doing nothing, but it's ridiculous how much fun I'm having. It's ridiculous how much fun I have with her *every time* we hang out.

Our first time getting together after we met at the pool hall, we went to the movies. We watched some mystery film, and I got to learn that Blair is one of those people who constantly says things in a frustrated voice when the actors' characters aren't being smart enough. People in the theater actually shushed her, but it only made me crack up.

Afterward, she apologized for her outbursts and explained how embarrassed she was, but that she just couldn't help it. I told her that I thought it was the most adorable thing in the world, and that was when we had our first kiss. She had to get up on her tippy toes.

It was weird and scary at first because I hadn't kissed anyone since Jennifer, but to my relief, kissing Blair felt like a totally different experience. She was sweet and shy and timid. She didn't immediately try to attack my face and jump my bones. It only lasted a couple seconds before she pulled away and had that adorable blush on her face.

It wasn't until the fourth time we hung out, when we went on a walk through the park by the college—where all the trees turned brilliant shades of orange, yellow, and red—that our kisses turned any more serious.

We had just finished cracking up about how pointless it was to go on a walk there because it was the end of November, and pretty much all the trees were bare of any leaves at all. Then we decided to have a leaf fight instead. We picked up all the dead, cracked, dry ones we could find and started tossing them at each other.

Then as we kept walking, we found a giant pile of leaves that some landscapers probably scraped together, and Blair and I fell back into it together. But then our heads collided, and we cried out in pain, and I rolled over on top of her to cradle her head and make sure she was okay. The way she stared at me was different that time. When I leaned forward and kissed her, she wrapped her hands tightly around my neck and pulled me in closer.

By the time we finished making out, I asked her if she had a concussion or something, because I definitely hadn't been expecting that.

Back in the kitchen, Blair's excited voice brings me back to the present. "Okay, are you ready for the secret ingredient?" She's looking at me from across the kitchen counter, her eyebrows wiggling.

"I love how excited you are about this," I tell her. Then my stomach twists at the fact that I said the word *love*.

If hers did, too, she doesn't show it. She reaches a hand into her reusable grocery bag, and when she pulls out the ingredient, I see that it is a can of cream of mushroom soup.

"Soup? That's a secret ingredient? What, are we supposed to dip the sandwiches in there or something?"

She slowly shakes her head at me like she wants me to guess again.

I scratch my head. "Uh, we heat that up? That way, we have backup when we try the Sloppy Joes and realize they taste disgusting?"

I know *that* won't be true because it smells amazing in here.

She smirks at me. "No." She digs around for a can opener, and then starts twisting the can open. "You mix it with the ground beef and tomato paste."

I look at her uncertainly.

"Come on, you trust me, don't you?"

My stomach dips so violently that I almost lose my appetite for a moment. Her dinner almost starts smelling repulsive.

Trust is a funny thing. How can I willingly give my trust, when the last person who had it was completely careless with it? And how is it fair to Blair for me *not* to give it to her, when she hasn't done anything to not deserve it? And what's even worse, is that I know she trusts me, but she shouldn't. Even a little bit. I'm not always honest. There's a lot I haven't told her about. There's a lot she doesn't know.

"Damascus?"

I shake my head quickly. Then I look into her beautiful eyes. Right now, they're widened in concern.

"Are... you... okay?" Clearly, she can sense she's triggered something. I wonder if I can play it off.

I grin at her and motion for her to continue with the soup can. "Go on, then. Let's see if it's as good as you say."

But she's not turning back around to the stove with it. She just stays there and stares at me with that questioning look. Then she bites her lower lip, and I know her well enough already to know that it's because she wants to say something but is afraid to do it.

I'm afraid to hear it.

"Blair, you're going to burn the meat."

She grips the edge of the counter. "Hey, I really like you, you know that?"

Butterflies swarm around in my stomach. "Oh, yeah?"

She nods her head. "And… I swear I didn't ask her to, but Sara did tell me a little bit about… your last girlfriend."

The only information I've ever divulged to Blair about Jennifer is that I just got dumped recently and didn't want to talk about it.

My face falls. "Oh, that's…" I don't really know what to say. Did it just get really hot in here?

"Um, I don't know that much, but I know that she hurt you."

I stand up from the stool, feeling antsy. "Yeah, Blair, we really don't have to talk about this."

"I know. I'm sorry, I haven't really hung around any other guys as much as I've hung around you. Like, ever."

I had moved to go get my glass of water off of the coffee table, but her words make me freeze. This is news to me. "I thought you said you have exes," I say.

"Well, kind of. I have guys whom I've gone on a couple dates with and stopped talking to after." She looks embarrassed. "And I'm not pretending I know what we're doing, or that I know what this is or how long it's going to last, but I just want you to know,"—she sets the can opener down on the counter and comes around the island to get closer to me—"I have no idea what I'm doing, but I *do* know that I'm never going to hurt you. I do know that I am nothing like her. And you can trust me."

"Damn," I breathe.

"What?" she asks shyly.

"I just… I've never had somebody be so straightforward with me." My heart is soaring. It's pounding in my ears and telling me that I don't have to be afraid to let Blair in all the way. That I can be honest and show her my entire true self, and that she might still accept me when I do.

But what if Blair is only saying this to the Damascus she knows *now?* What if she changes her mind when my *true* colors come out? Blair makes me want to be a better guy, but I can't promise that I will be. I have a darkness inside of me. I always have. I probably always will.

4

KENNETH

ork was insanely stressful today. Being a celebrity journalist is not always as it's cracked up to be. My boss, Rainer Wilkinson, had been calling me nonstop, asking me what I found out about Derek Heed, the college football player from a small town who has made fame mainly due to social media that my boss wants me to get a juicy story on for our magazine.

Rainer was thrilled to hear the news about someone

coming forward about Derek being abusive. I don't think it's necessarily something to be too happy about because women are in danger because of him, but Rainer has never really been one to have feelings.

When I unlock my front door and walk into my temporary housing not far from the stadium where Heed plays, courteous of Rainer, I'm feeling a little wary.

I set all of my belongings down on the dining table/workstation, then I head into my room to grab a towel so I can jump into the shower. But when I get to the bathroom in the hallway, I freeze. The door is closed, and there is light shining from underneath the crack of the door.

I can hear the shower running, so I set my towel back inside my bedroom and head to the living room to sit down on the couch and take a breather for a little bit. It is still so strange having someone—a *female* someone— who is practically a stranger, staying at my place.

Selena comes out of the bathroom about ten minutes later, wearing a fluffy robe and her hair up in a towel. She's wiping makeup off of her face with a fabric cloth, being careful around her black eye, and when she realizes I'm sitting there in the living room, she jumps and screams. It's as if *I'm* the one who is a surprising visitor in *her* home, not the other way around.

Her jumping and screaming only makes *me* jump and scream, too.

Then when we both calm down, we chuckle at each other.

"You scream like a legit girl," Selena tells me.

"What did you expect? You were screaming at me like I was an ax murderer. I thought maybe there was one standing behind me or something!"

We both laugh some more. It's true, though—whenever I legitimately scream, it tends to get a little high-pitched. I don't know how it happens, and I have no way of controlling it. It's actually pretty embarrassing. But at least I'm making Selena laugh. That's important.

"I'm sorry. I just wasn't expecting you home already," she says.

"Yeah… Well, work didn't exactly take long. Seeing as Derek is pretty much impossible to get in contact with." Not that I really want to get in contact with him right now. Not when I'm withholding his wife in my house. Already, I feel bad about even bringing it up.

Selena gets an uncomfortable look in her eye, and she turns away from me. I didn't mean to talk about it. I know she doesn't want to talk about him.

So, I change the subject, even though we can't avoid the topic of Derek in our conversation forever. He is the reason she's staying in my rental, after all. He is the reason I'm here in the first place. I keep my voice light. "Did you use up all the hot water? Because I was just about to hop in."

She turns back around to me and cringes.

"Oh, great, your guilty expression is *really* reassuring," I say. But I know she can see the twinkle in my eye.

"Why don't you get in, and I will boil a pot of water and toss it in as soon as it's ready? Does that work?" she teases back.

"You just want to get me to scream like that again," I banter.

She giggles and heads into the second bedroom to get changed. I've had to go out and buy her new clothes and toiletries because she doesn't want to be seen in public right now. I think I did a good job, but only because she was very specific with her shopping list.

I resume picking up my towel in my bedroom, along with a change of clothes, then I head to the bathroom. As soon as I close the door and lock it, she knocks on it.

"Yeah?" I call, my shirt already half off.

"Hey, is it okay if I make us dinner tonight? I noticed that you have some pasta noodles and sauce in your pantry."

I honestly don't member the last time somebody has cooked me anything. Spaghetti and marinara isn't the most difficult thing in the world to make, but it sounds ten times better when I don't have to be the one preparing it. I may not be thrilled to have Selena staying here with me right now, but at least I have a personal chef.

I think, for the briefest of moments, that I might really enjoy having Selena here. That this is the start of a long-lasting friendship. I haven't had too many of those in my life. But Selena and I have been brought together in the wildest of ways. Surely, it means the base of a solid foundation for our relationship. *Platonic* relationship.

"Go crazy," I tell her.

WHEN I GET out of the shower, I open the door in my towel, and I am greeted by the heavenly scent of the warmed-up pasta sauce. I get those eight-dollar jars at the grocery store, none of that simple canned stuff.

Then I remember that I'm in my towel, even though I brought my clothes into the bathroom to get changed, so I quickly re-close the door before Selena sees me like this. Then I put my t-shirt and joggers on and walk out, barefoot, into the kitchen.

"How is the water?" she asks me right away.

Her back is to me, and she is dumping the pasta into the strainer in the sink. She hadn't bothered to blow dry her hair, so it's stringy and dangling above her shoulders. It's weird to see her in such a natural state like this. Had I never discovered Derek abusing her, I wouldn't have ever gotten to know her this closely. This quickly, either. But I like it.

She finally turns to me, and I get a good look at her black eye now that she doesn't have any makeup covering it. It's still really bad, but it's definitely healing. Every time I look at it, I get this twisting feeling in my stomach like I just want to run out of this house, find where Derek lives, and bash his brains in with a bat. How can any man think it's okay to put their hand on a woman? Especially one they claim to love.

"Can you not, like, stare at it?" she asks me, catching me in the act. I quickly cover my eyes with both hands like I've just seen her naked.

"Oh, God, I'm so sorry. I didn't mean to! This is so embarrassing!" I stumble around the kitchen, pretending to bump into things, but then I accidentally do ram my hip into the edge of the counter really hard. I double over and cry out in pain, and it makes her laugh. That was the goal. Keeping a smile on Selena's face has quickly become one of my favorite hobbies.

"No, I'm actually being serious," I tell her, gasping. "I didn't mean to do that."

She walks over to me, still laughing. "I know! That's what makes it even funnier!" She puts her hands on my shoulders and steadies me, and I'm allowed to remove my hands from my eyes now, I think.

I lift the hem of my shirt up, and we look at my side together—it's already red and puffy, definitely going to bruise. She frowns at it and crosses her arms. "Want me to get you a baggie of ice?"

In my head, I begin replaying the scene of the night she ended up at my doorstep, when I had been the one getting her ice for her wound. I don't like thinking about it.

I shake it off and walk over to sit down at the table. "Thanks for your half-sincere concern," I say.

She finishes getting everything ready, then we serve ourselves our plates, and we sit at the table, pushing my work stuff aside, and together, we enjoy a quiet, peaceful meal. Derek isn't brought up again.

5

———

DAMASCUS

Six months ago…

I don't even want to be at this stupid support group right now. There's absolutely no point in it.

No, wait, I take that back. There's *one* point—so I can yell at everyone and help explain to them how pointless this all is, too.

"You okay, Damascus?" the leader asks me about ten

minutes into the session. Apparently, she can see the hate in my eyes.

"You don't look so good," Terrance comments.

I cross my arms and extend my feet out in the crappy, old folding chair I'm sitting in. "Oh, you know," I start with a shrug. "Just dandy. Except for the fact that this group is fucking stupid, and there's no reason for any of us to be here."

Some people gasp. The support group leader tilts her head and stares at me like a concerned mother, even though she can't even be that much older than me. What makes her want to do this stupid job, anyway? Does it even pay well? Does she even meet the correct qualifications? What is she supposed to do when someone like me comes in and has a meltdown like this?

"Why do you think you feel that way right now?" the woman asks me, crossing her legs.

"Why do you think?" I snap at her. I'm just so angry that I can't help it. I know I normally like her. I don't know why right now, I wouldn't care if she were dead. "Aren't you supposed to help tell *me* that?"

"Maybe you should step out into the hall and take a second," Shannon tries. I want to walk over to her and push her off of her stupid chair.

"Damascus, has something happened?" the leader asks.

Her voice is soft and worried now. It makes me stop for a second. It's rare that I ever meet anyone who actually cares about me. Jennifer had been the only one I thought did. But as it turns out, everything about Jennifer had all been a lie. No one cares. What's the point of being alive if no one even cares whether you exist?

I stand up. "This class is complete bullshit," I say darkly. "You're all lying to yourselves if you think it's helping anything. It's not. You're all doomed, or you're all doomed to lose someone. Just accept it and move the fuck on." I stomp out of the room. Normally, my boots don't make much noise when I walk, but it's so dead quiet after my outburst that everyone can hear every single one of my steps as I leave.

6

———

GISELLE

I'm worried it's going to feel weird when I go hang out with Eliza next. After the charity gala, I almost didn't even expect her to want to reach out to me again. She seemed so thrown off by the fact that I have a boyfriend now. She seemed completely uncomfortable just being around me at all. I was just beginning to think that our secret kiss had ruined our relationship. I spent days hitting myself on the head, wishing I could take it all back.

I love Eliza as a person. I don't ever want to not have her in my life. I was fine keeping her as a friend. I hadn't even been the one who kissed her! Did I think about it? *Yes*. But I didn't do it. I didn't want to hurt Shawn like that. I *don't* want to hurt Shawn like that. Especially not when the poor guy has ALS and will soon be confined to a wheelchair.

Ugh, sometimes I just feel like I've made such a mess of things.

But at least it's not totally ruined.

Eliza has invited me out to lunch. So, here I am, sitting on the patio of this incredibly adorable café in LA. All the tables and chairs are made of white wood, and there are cute yellow umbrellas with white stripes over every table. The centerpiece is always a small bouquet of red roses. It looks like something out of a fairytale story.

When Eliza sees me, she's waves, but I can't exactly tell what her expression is because she has on her giant sunglasses, and her bodyguards are almost blocking my view. When she is safely at the table in front of me, she finally takes off the shades.

My stomach has been in knots since yesterday morning when she first invited me, but when I look at her sweet, casual smile, I instantly feel more at ease. Things don't have to be weird. We can just resume our friendship as if nothing ever happened. I know we can.

"Hi, love what you've done with your hair," Eliza starts off by telling me. "Is it lighter, too, or just shorter?"

I giggle. "Oh, all I did was trim it."

Leave it to *her* to notice when I got barely half an inch trimmed from my mane. But her noticing it is also just letting me know that she clearly pays attention to details. That she pays attention to what I look like and notices when I make changes. But I shouldn't think too hard about that, should I?

A waitress comes by looking like she's doing everything in her power not to burst out into an excited scream. It makes me wonder which one of us she's obsessed with, and if she had to ask one of her coworkers to take this table instead of them. "What can I start you lovely ladies off with to drink today?"

I let Eliza go first.

"Gin martini, dry, filthy. Two olives." She looks tired when she says it, like it's desperately needed to give her a little pick-me-up.

"Um, I would love an unsweetened iced tea, please. Green, if you have it." As good as a real drink sounds right now, I have to stay as anti-bloated as possible for an upcoming show.

The waitress walks away with a huge grin on her face, and Eliza sighs. "I honestly don't know how you do it. It must be excruciating not getting to drink when you feel like it."

I give her a shrug. "Maybe sometimes. But I also love my job and don't want to do anything to jeopardize it. So, if I have to be sober, so be it."

I kid you not. I stare at her and watch as her eyes flutter to my lips, down the front of my torso, up to what she can see before the table, and then back to my eyes. I'm pretty sure Eliza just checked me out.

And I'm pretty sure I liked it.

We go about our lunch; I order a boring salad with no dressing, and Eliza gets herself a healthy-looking meatless sandwich. We both nibble and talk about only the casual stuff. She whines to me about work. I joke around with her and get her to smile. One smile from Eliza makes my entire day. Always.

But of course, we couldn't just stay on simple conversation topics forever. Eliza wipes her mouth with her yellow cloth napkin and looks at me with an expression I can't quite determine. But there's still a small smile on her face, too.

"So, I must say, I am very happy for you and your mystery boyfriend, whoever he may be."

I would've been a fool to think that she would never bring this up. No matter how much I don't want to talk about it.

I tuck some loose hair strands behind my ear and look away from her briefly. "Oh, yeah… Thank you. He is—he's great. This is just what I need right now."

I didn't want to say it, but I had to. It's the truth. This *is* for the best. I could never be with Eliza, and Eliza could never be with me. I don't want the public to know I like women because I don't want to lose my fans, and I don't want to lose my job. I don't want to go back to being a nobody.

Do I want a boyfriend? Especially the one I don't have?

No.

She takes a sip of her martini, and that sip slowly turns into her draining the rest of it and waving our excited waitress back over to get her another one. After that, she crosses her arms on her lap and leans back against her chair. "So, I don't suppose you're ready to tell me who he is yet?" she asks.

That is exactly the last thing I want to do. I don't want her to know. Ever. But I know I'm being ridiculous. I know it's inevitable.

I cringe. "Not yet, if that's okay. It's not that I don't trust you, I just don't know if it's even gonna last, so I don't want to talk about it too much yet until I know it's real."

I pulled that excuse right out of my butt. Maybe I should take up acting, too, because this performance is miraculous.

Eliza nods her head, but her eyes have a faraway look in them, like she's thinking about something deeply.

"Liza?" I ask. "Is everything okay?"

It's a terrifying question to ask because I have no idea what her answer is going to be. We didn't exactly talk about what happened in the stairwell that day. Not once. Not after she told me it would never happen again. I don't know if this is the moment that she's going to bring it up again. Or if she is going to bring up something worse. I don't know how I'm going to react to whatever it is she's about to say to me.

All I know is I'm suddenly terrified.

She looks back at me, and for a second, it almost seems like she forgot that I was even here. "Oh, yes, I'm fine."

But I know Eliza well enough now to know when she's not being honest with me.

"No, I don't think you are." I put my hand out on the table, but I don't reach out to her, as much as I would love to. "You can talk to me. You know you can." I almost want to pull my hand back away because I don't want her to notice how it has suddenly gone all clammy and jittery with my nerves. I can just sense that something is off.

She tenses her jaw and seems to be deep in thought again, clearly contemplating over whether she can confide in me with whatever it is she wants to get off her chest. Then her martini arrives, and she takes two sips. When she sets it down, she seems ready.

"I guess I'm still just having a really hard time with Shawn," she begins. "He pushed away his kids because of his disease. He doesn't want them seeing him like this. He doesn't want to be remembered this way by them. I guess I always wondered why he wasn't doing the same to me, but with his recent doctor's visit, I'm beginning to think he might finally be doing so." She puts her elbow on the table and rests her temple on her pointer and middle fingers.

"What's he been doing?"

I feel horrible. All she does is spend most of her day when she's not at work at home taking care of him. Whatever Shawn may be going through, it doesn't make it okay for him to push her away. He needs her, and he knows it.

And as horrible as it sounds, I am relieved that the thing she wanted to talk about was Shawn. Maybe we will never talk about the kiss ever again.

It's for the best.

It has to be.

"Well, he told me he wants his own bedroom in the house. That he doesn't think we should have to sleep in the same bed, in the same room, when his new bed gets put in. And he's spending a bunch of his time locked up in his studio, even though I know he's not painting anything. I've tried to check on him before, but he told me to never interrupt him when he's in his studio and didn't open the door, so I had no choice but to leave him locked alone in there. It was quite terrifying, actually. What if something had happened to him? How would any of us have gotten to him? I feel like a complete bitch, but I almost want to have all the locks removed around our house. At least on the inside."

"That's tough. And *completely* unfair of him. But I know he loves you, and you know he loves you, too. Maybe he just needs some time."

"That's what I thought about his kids, but he's had the diagnosis for quite some time now, and he still hasn't wanted to see or talk to them."

"Why does he like to hang out with me?" I can't help asking.

"Because you've only known him like this. He's partial to people who only met him after his diagnosis. He feels like he can be more himself around them. He doesn't feel like he has to try so hard to be who he was before."

This info saddens me to my core. Then I'm cut even deeper when Eliza's eyes well up with tears, a normally rare thing occurring *yet again* within the span of just a few short weeks.

"Not only does Shawn like having you around, Giselle, but *I* like having you around, too. I… I need you around."

It shouldn't, but her words make me swoon.

"I'm not going anywhere, Liza," I reassure her.

Dang it, how *badly* I wish I could just stroke her arm. Pat the top of her hand. Bump her foot with mine. But being outside on a patio in LA means free shows for passersby and the paparazzi. And Eliza has to know that I don't feel for her that way. Even if it's a lie.

Because I am pretty sure I'm crazy about her.

"I know I have Shawn, but I really feel completely alone." Eliza takes more big gulps of her drink. She has barely touched her food.

"You're not alone," I say. "You are one of my closest friends. I'm not going anywhere."

"Friends," she repeats, nodding her head slowly and not looking at me. I'd give anything to know what she's thinking right now. Could she possibly be thinking about how she wishes we were more? More like I wish we could be, despite everything?

The last thing I want to do is make things harder on Eliza. I just want her to be happy. I don't want her to have to deal with any more drama in her life. So, I have to be her friend. I can *only* be her friend.

That has to be that. Any more romantic thoughts of Eliza have to flee my mind. I have to be done with my wishes and fantasies.

From this moment on, Eliza and I will remain friends and nothing more.

It's in both of our best interests.

7

———

BRENNAN

I've tried messaging Leah on Facebook. And Instagram. And even Twitter. In fact, I made a Twitter account just so I *could* message her.

I figure—desperate times call for desperate measures.

But she didn't reply to any of them. She doesn't want to talk to me, and I'm not really sure I know why.

I know we weren't exactly close in high school, but I wasn't mean to her. I do know of a way I could probably get her cell phone number, but I don't want to completely creep her out, and I don't really want anybody knowing what I'm up to.

But the thing is, it's been a couple weeks now since the anonymous post was made about Derek. And since then, more have come out. All of them are anonymous. Some of them claim not to be the same person.

I know some of them *have* to be fake—just people trying to join into the drama. But the more I read about it, the more stressed out I become. I'm not sure what to think. I don't think Derek would ever intentionally hurt somebody, but I guess I've never been the one who's in a relationship with him. He beat me up growing up, but I figured that was just what older brothers did.

I've tried to talk to Derek a few times, but he doesn't seem interested. He keeps telling me he just has a lot going on, and that he will text me later. But of course, he never does.

I figure my only other option is to try Henderson's.

This might be kind of outrageous, but if I'm going to talk to Leah—which I desperately want to do—then I figure my next best chance of getting to do so is by running into her again like I had there.

So, I block out an entire day. I don't even go to the office or to disc golf.

I head to Henderson's when they open—which is nine in the morning for some ridiculous reason—and I sit at the bar all damn day. She had seemed like such a regular when she was here before, so she has to come back in eventually. I'll stay here all day, every day until she does, if I have to.

"It's not usually like you to be in here this long," Jane notices. I've been pacing myself on the alcohol, at least. This is only my fifth beer and second shot, and I've been here all day.

"Just kind of tough being at home right now," I tell her. I always sit at the bar when I come in, so I've gotten pretty close with Jane.

"Yeah, I get that…" Jane trails off. She's shining some glasses with a clean white towel. "But your entire body is facing the door, and you keep staring at it with a really intense look on your face."

"So?"

I'm only partially listening. I'm still waiting for Leah to show up.

"So, you're obviously waiting for someone?"

Damn, she has gotten to know me too well in the short few weeks that I've been coming here.

"Oh, I don't know. Maybe. I'm not trying to get my hopes up."

She checks her watch and looks back at me. "Brennan, you've been here for *nine* hours. I am going to go on a limb and say you definitely do have your hopes up." She chuckles a little but is also giving me an incredulous stare.

I sigh. Maybe I should leave, but I'm just worried that the second I do is when she's going to walk in. I owe it to Derek to figure out what's happening around here. I want to know why people are saying these things about him.

It's eleven o'clock when I finally give up and decide to call it a night. I pay my tab, which has racked up considerably because I got hungry and needed to eventually eat.

Jane gives me a sympathetic head shake, and I wave her goodbye and head to the exit.

When I put my coat on and step out into the freezing cold air, there she is.

Leah Olson. She just hopped out of a rideshare and is heading toward the entrance. Heading toward me. She likes to look down when she walks, so she nearly collides with me before she looks up and realizes who the person standing in front of her is.

She gives me a startled, horrified look like I'm the last person in the world she wants to run into. I don't like it, and I don't understand it.

"Leah, hey," I start.

She turns and looks back at her rideshare as it drives away, and I get the feeling that she was hoping she could just climb right back inside of it.

"Brennan."

I scratch the back of my head. "Uh, I've been trying to get a hold of you these past couple of weeks," I say. "I was hoping to talk to you about something."

She swallows audibly, takes a deep breath, and raises her chin up a little bit.

"I've heard the news, Brennan," she admits, "and if it's okay with you, I don't want to talk to you."

She goes to step around me, but I block her path.

I don't like the way it makes her look… afraid of me.

She recoils and steps back.

"I don't understand," I say to her. "What have I ever done to you? I only want to ask you some questions about it. You dated Derek in high school."

"What, you want to know if *I'm* one of the many women who have made an anonymous post about him?" She crosses her arms and challenges me. The cold air outside is making her already pale skin look ghostly, and her long brown hair is framing her face and forming a small curtain for her to hide behind.

"I'm not here to accuse you of anything, Leah. This is just… it's kind of messing up my family, you know? I'm just trying to get everything straight."

"Have you been, like, waiting for me here?"

"Well, you wouldn't answer any of my messages."

"Yeah, and I thought that would've given you the hint." She tries to go around me again, but I have to step in front of her path again. I can't let the conversation end like this. I have to get answers. I have to know what the fuck is going on.

She growls and steps back from me again. "I don't trust you. And I don't trust your family."

This makes my stomach stink, and my mouth goes dry. "Why don't you trust us? Why don't you trust *me*? You don't even know me."

"I know you well enough. Especially if you're Derek Heed's brother."

I stick my hands into the pockets of my jeans. "Okay, that's not really fair." Just because I'm related to Derek doesn't mean I'm like him. Before tonight, I had always wanted to be him, though.

She looks away from me, her jaw tense.

So, I continue. "Just—did Derek—You know… do anything to you while you were together?"

My heart is beating so fast that I think it might fly right out of my chest. I just hope she's willing to answer the question. I hope this is it. This is the moment where I get to decide to fully commit to being on my brother's team, or reevaluate the situation entirely.

"Brennan, please, let me pass."

"Why won't you just tell me?" I beg. My voice is growing angry, but I'm trying not to let it. "Leah, if he did something to you, I need to know."

"Well, I'm not gonna talk to you about it. Besides, how should I know you and your family aren't just trying to keep me quiet?"

My mouth hangs open as her words slam into me. They send my whole world twisting on its axis. All of my ideals of Derek. All of my thoughts and opinions. In a single second, they do a one eighty.

Seeing the expression on my face, Leah sighs. She knows she's told me all I need to hear. Even if she didn't mean to.

It's like I have completely turned to stone as the rest of the world continues to whirl around me in a dizzying blur. I feel sick. My lungs have stopped working. The strength to hold myself upright has become almost over-whelming. I don't want it to be true. I desperately need it *not* to be.

But it is. And there is nothing I can do to change it.

Everything those women have been saying. All of those anonymous posts. They weren't lying. My brother—my best friend—my idol—is a monster.

8

———

KENNETH

*D*erek Heed does a pretty damn good job acting like an innocent victim in all of this. Day after day, I keep heading to the stadium, getting interviews with anyone who will let me. I don't know who Derek hired or what he's promising people, but I can't find anyone but Selena to back me up on these allegations, and I'm not allowed to interview her on record.

None of Derek's teammates seem to have a single

bad word to say about him. The only statements that Derek has released to the press are about how he's not sure who is making these claims, but that they are false. The only thing that seems to have people questioning him is the fact that Selena hasn't made a single appearance to the public ever since the night she showed up at my house.

Yeah. Selena's been at my house for a while now. She's more than welcome, of course. Her parents live across the country, and she doesn't know anyone else in town. And I honestly would hold her hostage if she tried to go back to *her* house. Fine—not really, but I'm just worried about her.

I don't know. She's possibly the sweetest, funniest, most thoughtful woman I've ever met, and the thought of her spending the last five years trapped with a master manipulator, who has everyone in his life fooled, breaks my heart.

She's the last person who deserves this. And I don't know any of Derek Heed's exes, but I know they don't deserve this, either.

No one knows Selena is with me. According to what I've seen online and have been told by the coach and the team, Selena has been staying at home, out of the drama, because while these allegations are false, Selena doesn't want to seem like she's not an advocate for domestic abuse.

I even tried calling out to Derek the other day—after they won a game, and he came walking through the stadium hallways with a huge cocky grin on his face—to see if he knew where Selena was. He had snapped his head to me so quickly that I almost wondered if he broke his neck. Then the smile was wiped off his face, and he shoulder-checked me as he passed by, obviously refusing to comment.

I do wonder where he thinks she's hiding, though. And I hope he never figures out that it's my place. I want to keep Selena safe for as long as possible.

It's freezing when I get home from the college early this evening. It's cloudy and windy out, and even though it's not overcast, I wonder if it's going to rain.

I get out of my Subaru and head to the front door, but my phone rings in my pocket, and I pause.

When I pull it out, I see Rainer's name on the screen.

Not what I need right now.

"Hey," I say.

"Where's my story?"

Hello to you too, boss. No, I'm great, thanks for asking. How are you?

"Still working on it." I don't mean to show attitude, but he can be such a jerk sometimes that it's really difficult not to.

My boss' voice is intimidating and threatening, as usual. "This was your chance to make things right, Kenneth; don't you forget," he begins. "I keep waiting to see if I find out that another magazine has gotten an exclusive interview with his wife or one of his old girl-friends. You're lucky I haven't."

I chew on my tongue, biting down so hard that it's painful. I wish I could explain to him the stressful situation I'm in.

"I'll get you your exclusive. I assure you."

"Let me make myself very clear to you, Kenny."

I look up at the sky and wish to be struck by lightning.

"If you don't get me a story before anyone else, you can kiss your job goodbye. I've given you plenty of time."

Stones drop in my stomach. I clench my phone tightly, thinking I might throw it.

"Do you understand me?" he asks when I don't answer right away.

"Yes, I understand," I say with a hoarse voice.

He hangs up, and I have to wait outside for a bit so I can compose myself. I'm so angry that I don't even feel cold. I look toward the one window at the front of my house. The blinds are closed, but I can tell the light is on.

What am I going to do? My job is everything.

I finally go inside. Selena is sitting on the couch, messaging someone on her phone. I can't help but wonder if she's spilling details of her abuse to someone besides me.

Her entire face brightens when she sees me, but then falls when she sees the expression I probably have on my face.

"Kenny?" she asks, clicking her phone off and getting to her feet.

"You okay?" I ask her before she can ask me.

She nods. "He keeps making fake Instagram accounts and trying to message me, but he's not being mean because he knows I could just use it against him."

She looks nervous, though, like she isn't sure she would use the messages against him if given the option.

I nod my head, my jaw tense, and look away from her, into the kitchen. She has a pot of something being kept warm on the stove. It smells delicious, but I don't have much of an appetite.

She walks behind me and over to the window in front of the dining table. Then she cracks open the blinds.

"Making sure no one followed me back?" I ask her, dumping some of my stuff onto the table like I always do when I come home.

Standing next to me, she quickly grabs my wrist. "Kenny, it's snowing!"

I furrow my eyebrows.

I literally just walked in twenty seconds ago. How had I missed it?

Selena opens the front door and steps out onto the porch to look at it.

My stomach plummets as I follow after her. "Selena," I warn. I don't want anyone to recognize her.

"It's fine," she argues. I'm about to protest, but the fat flakes make me forget about it. Already, they're sticking to the ground.

I don't live where it snows anymore. It's kind of mesmerizing to see.

Selena hugs herself because of the cold. Her bare feet are standing on the porch, and I don't know how they haven't turned into icicles yet.

"You know what we should do?" she asks, looking away from the snow for one second to set her eyes on mine. I can't help but notice how beautiful she looks out here, so vulnerable and happy about the snow, sort of like a little kid. The bruise on her eye has nearly gone away, too.

"What?"

"We should buy some Christmas decorations. Hang them up. Make this place a little cheerier."

I hesitate.

"Come on! Kenny, I know it's just a rental, but who cares? Living in a rental and not knowing how long you're going to stay isn't a reason *not* to celebrate Christmas."

As much as I want to be frustrated with her, as angry as I am at my boss, and as scared as I am about losing my job, I can't help but feel a little bit lighter. Something about being around Selena just does that to me.

I crack a small smile. "Oh, what the heck."

Selena squeals excitedly and throws her arms around me in a hug. I am not used to being hugged by her, so my body tenses up a little at first. When she seems to remember that she hasn't ever hugged me either, she pauses briefly, and then steps away.

"I'm coming with," she tells me.

"No, Selena."

She rolls her eyes. "I'll wear a hoodie and keep sunglasses on. You do the same. No one will recognize either of us. Besides, it's late. No one is probably even out right now. Especially in the snow. Come on!"

She dashes back inside the house before I could even answer her. I chew on the inside of my cheeks nervously. If somebody catches me with Selena, I get the feeling that they're going to spread rumors that I kidnapped her. That there's no way she would be staying here, hidden, willingly.

And what if my boss finds out?

Selena quickly gets changed and meets me back out on the porch, where I haven't moved. When she sees the look on my face, she tilts her head. "Kenny?"

I suck in a breath and shake my keys at her. "Let's go," I say to her.

We get into my Subaru and head to a supermarket, both of us wearing our disguises when we enter the store. Selena was right; the store is completely dead. Not even the workers really seem to be lingering around.

So, Selena and I go to the Christmas section and start browsing through the decorations, the two of us even managing to crack jokes and laugh with each other as we do so. The more time I spend with Selena, the more I wonder why anyone would want to hurt her. She's literally perfect.

And really hard to be mad at, might I add.

After we've selected our lights, ribbons, Christmas tree, and ornaments, we go to pay at the self-checkout—that way, we don't have to talk to anybody—then we get back into my car and head back to my rental.

"Look at that," Selena comments as she helps me get the stuff out of my trunk. "We weren't spotted once!"

It's around seven at night now, but even though the snow is falling heavily, and we can barely see, Selena is determined to hang up the decorations right now. So together, we line the roof of the rental and the porch railing with red and green strands of lights, then when we're nearly about to freeze our asses off, we head inside and get to work on the Christmas tree.

"I don't want to freak you out, but I left the stove on warm the entire time we were gone…" Selena says to me, biting her bottom lip as she looks over into the kitchen.

I look over at the pot on the stove. Indeed, the stove light is on.

I rush over to it and open the lid. I had expected such an old stove to have burned the shit out of whatever's inside, but to my surprise, the soup that Selena made is gently bubbling and still smells as heavenly as ever.

"Looks like we're good," I tell her.

"I only had a little bit earlier, but I definitely want more. Do you want to eat dinner together after this?"

"Yeah, I do. Thank you for cooking. You really don't have to do it *every* day. I can pick us up takeout or something for a change."

Selena shrugs and goes back to hanging up some glittery silver ornaments on the tree. "I need something to keep me busy."

I nod at her, understanding all too well. Then we resume decorating the tree together, Christmas music playing in the background, the two of us a little bit quieter and less giggly than we had been at the supermarket.

I just like the way Selena's face glows from the lights of the Christmas tree. I like how it feels like I'm doing an actual Christmas tradition for once. I know Selena and I aren't romantic with each other, but if she were my girlfriend, this would be one hell of a romantic evening.

When we sit down for dinner later, we quietly sip our chicken noodle soup, made completely from scratch.

Selena's feet are up on her chair, her knees tucked into her as she bends over them to eat her dinner. She keeps looking at me every so often, and I can't help but wonder what she's thinking.

"So, how are you doing with everything?" I ask her.

"What do you mean?"

"Uh, I guess I just want to know what your plan is. Do you have one?"

I have no idea how long Selena plans on staying at my rental with me—it's not exactly a question I've brought up yet. But we have to figure it out at some point. The longer she stays here, the harder I feel like it's going to be to let her leave.

"I'm just not ready," she tells me. "But I really appreciate everything you've been doing for me."

I nod at her and sip my soup some more.

"Are you really ever going to be ready, though?" I ask her. "Is anybody?"

She lets her soup spoon fall into the soup bowl. "What are you trying to say?"

I grip my spoon tighter in my hand. "I was just thinking… Maybe it's time you finally come forward about writing that post."

We had worked together to figure out how to come forward about Derek's attacks. Selena had made it very clear that she was too afraid to come out and talk about it herself, so I was the one who told her she could make an anonymous post, and not reference herself as Derek's wife. She could just say she was one of his ex-girlfriends. Both of us had no doubt that he'd been abusive in his previous relationships also.

Selena's face falls, and it makes my heart sink. "I don't know what will happen to me if I do that," she explains. "I don't know if I *can* do it. I thought you understood that."

"So… what? You're just gonna live here in my rental until I have to go back to LA, then you're gonna find some other person's house to hide out in? Become homeless? Change your name and move to a different country? I mean, come on, Selena." I'm not trying to get so worked up, but I can't help it. I'm not even sure why. But right now, it doesn't feel like it's because of my job.

Selena sighs and pushes her bowl away like she's done eating.

"You don't have to stop eating. I'm sorry if I'm upsetting you."

She looks away from me and doesn't respond.

But then, sitting there and staring at her, my blood slightly boiling, it hits me. The reason why I'm so worked up.

"I need to ask you to do something," I begin.

She clenches her jaw when she looks back at me. "I'm not going to admit that I wrote that post, Kenny."

I shake my head and lick my lips. "Not that. Although, I really think you should," I say. "I'm asking you, as a friend, as someone who cares a great deal about you even though I really don't know you that well, to leave Derek Heed. File for divorce. Get a restraining order. Get out of that marriage, and get away from him. As far away as possible. I know you can do it. I know it's scary, and you don't know what's going to happen, but anything, I promise you, is better than being stuck in a marriage with a man who hurts you."

I'm not sure what I was expecting her to say in return, but I definitely wasn't expecting her to burst into sobs.

Selena pushes her chair back so quickly that it nearly falls over, then she dashes into her bedroom and closes the door.

I sit there at the table, still clenching my spoon, my heart pounding in my ears.

Again, I can't help but ask myself.

What the hell am I going to do?

9

GISELLE

*E*liza and I are hanging out again. Today, we are shopping for Christmas presents—I'm getting stuff for my family, and she's getting stuff for hers.

We are in this cute part of LA where every single store for blocks has completely changed their inventory to only Christmas-themed things, like decorations, red and green pajama outfits for the whole family, and all the top choices on everybody's Christmas lists.

The weather outside is an almost chilly sixty-nine

degrees, the sun is shining brilliantly, and Eliza and I look stylish as ever while our bodyguards clear the stores before we enter so that we can shop in private.

I made sure that Lonnie and Bryan explained to the store workers that we promise to spend a lot of money so that they don't feel bad for kicking everyone else out. Neither of us really feel like giving out autographs to fans today.

Sometimes I prefer to walk around in a disguise, so I'm less recognized, and I make my bodyguard look like my boyfriend or friend, but being around Eliza, I want to look my best. I want her to be attracted to me and regret telling me that she never meant to kiss me.

"Did I tell you?" I ask her as we browse the aisles of Christmas ornaments in one shop.

Eliza is holding a Snoopy-themed ornament and smiling to herself. "Tell me what?"

I don't look at her when I say it. "I've been thinking of heading home for the holiday. My family has been dying to see me, and if I don't, I'll never hear the end of it."

Naturally, I'm hoping this makes her sad. I'm hoping she gets jealous that I'm going to be with my family instead of with her and Shawn.

I hope she asks me to stay.

Instead, she turns her body toward me and beams at me. "I think that's a lovely idea. At least your parents *want* to spend time with their children."

I know that's a dig at Shawn, and that she is still feeling bitter that for yet another holiday, Shawn is insisting that his kids don't pay him a visit.

I grab Eliza's shoulder and give it a squeeze. "Maybe he will come around?" I try. "There's still time, you know." Christmas isn't for another week.

"I know, but I just don't have any kids of my own to spoil. And it wouldn't be the same just shipping off some presents to them and not getting to see their reaction." Eliza sighs, putting the Snoopy ornament in her little shopping basket and continuing down the aisle. My bodyguards, Lonnie and Bryan, are hanging out by the front door, while her bodyguard, Victor, is browsing the store himself.

I have no idea what it's like to be in Eliza's shoes, and I can't even fathom the idea of having stepchildren. In fact, I'm not sure if kids have ever been in my cards. So, not knowing how to reply to her, I shrug and keep browsing the store. I still have yet to find the perfect gift.

Eliza trails along behind me, stopping every so often to look at another ornament. She has been really sad lately about everything with her husband, but today is the first time I've gotten genuine smiles out of her.

"So, will you be bringing Steve with you, then?" Eliza asks me. This makes me stop moving. She wants to know about Steve? Why would she care?

I turn around to her and give her a bright smile. "I think so! If I can convince him, that is."

"Does Steve really need convincing?"

She *does* have a point; Steve is incredibly in love with me. I'm pretty sure he would do anything I asked of him. Well… almost anything.

I shrug. "Probably not. You're right. He's just nervous meeting my family for the first time, that's all.

I've never brought a guy home before. So, I'm kind of nervous, too."

"Steve is a wonderful guy. I'm really glad I introduced you two," Eliza tells me. I sense something else behind her words, something insincere and bitter. But maybe I'm just crazy.

"Yeah. Thank you," I say as we move to the next aisle. "I'm sorry it took me so long to tell you and Shawn about him. I just didn't know if it was going to work out, and I didn't want to get your hopes up. I know how much you would love for me to end up with a guy like him, right?" I look over my shoulder to peek back at her, and I find that her lips are pursed and her eyes are squinted.

So, I stop browsing again and turn to her. "What?" I ask, my heart skipping a beat. Doesn't she like Steve? Doesn't she want me to be with somebody? Doesn't she want me to be happy?

Eliza is silent for a long while, pondering something deeply. But then she waves her hand in front of my face and finally looks at me. "Oh, don't look at me like that, Giselle."

"Look at you like what?"

She steps closer to me and leans in like what she's about to say, she doesn't want to be overheard by her bodyguard or the store workers. "Fine, if you must know," she begins, "that day in the stairwell… Well, if it wasn't obvious, I realized that I might have very confusing feelings for you."

My mouth drops open. I'm so stunned that I can't

even find the words to reply with. All I can do is stare at her, gaping.

"Oh, come on, Giselle. I'm not an idiot. I know you knew this. Don't look so surprised. Besides, it's not like anything could happen. You understand that, right? Even if it was in private. I… I'm never going to leave my husband. And it just…" She stops talking so she can giggle nervously. "Well, it would never work. It would be far too complicated, especially given who we are in this industry."

She seems like she's ready to be done with the conversation as she steps away and resumes browsing through some expensive soaps, but I'm not done.

"Eliza… I—"

She interrupts. "I'm happy you're with Steve. It's the way things are supposed to be. Especially if you're happy."

10

———

BRENNAN

I have absolutely zero plan as I drive to my brother's house. I have no idea what I'm gonna say to him, and I have no idea what he's going to say back.

He's my *brother*. I'm supposed to have his back. I know that's what he'll think. I know he'll expect me to take his side. To say everyone else is lying.

I just can't do that. I no longer believe him.

I enter the code to his gated house and drive up the

circular driveway. Then I put my car in park and climb out, my head spinning as I make my way to his front door.

When I pound on it and turn to look back at my car, I can see another vehicle parked outside of the gate. It's probably the paparazzi, or maybe even another woman whom Derek is beating up.

When I hear the door unlock and open, I turn back to it. There he is. He stands shirtless and sweaty before me, like he was just running on the treadmill, and his face bursts into a wide grin when he realizes it's me.

That grin.

It does something to me.

"Hey, little bro—"

Before I can let him finish his sentence, I punch him square in the jaw. Of course, he only stumbles back a little bit; he's much stronger than me, and I don't get a lot of practice punching people. Unlike him.

Derek gets a wild look in his eyes as his face turns red, and he grabs his jaw. "What the fuck was that?"

But I don't want to talk. So, I step inside his front door and punch him again, this time, in the stomach. He doubles over, but only for a moment. Then he lets out a raging roar and tackles me, and the both of us fly out his front door and tumble onto his lawn.

Maybe it's the fact that I did wrestling in high school and he didn't, but I'm somehow able to roll myself on top of him. Then I deliver another blow. Right to his temple.

"Brennan! Stop!" Derek cries underneath me. Then his lip splits when I punch him again. "Are you crazy?!"

I can barely hear what he is saying. I can barely control what I'm doing. All I know is that I'm angry. All I know is that I want him to pay. That I don't want him to get away with this.

"What the hell is wrong with you?" I yell as I punch him again. It hurts my hand like hell, and I finally roll off of him. He's in too much pain to try to get back at me, so we both lie there on the grass in agony.

My face feels wet, so I touch my cheek to see if it's Derek's blood, but when I pull my hand away, I realize it's a tear. I don't even know when I started crying.

"Brennan," Derek manages to croak.

Right now, there's nothing he could say to me. And I realize as I slowly get to my feet, that there's nothing I want to say to him, either. Nothing I do is going to change what he's already done.

11

———

DAMASCUS

I never thought I would be one of those people who goes to an ice-skating rink around Christmas time with their significant other.

But yet, somehow, here I am. At an ice-skating rink. With my significant other.

Although, the *being with my significant other* part isn't so bad. Blair and I became official just yesterday. She had been pretty adamant during our late-night phone call about determining what our label was. She said she wouldn't be satisfied if she didn't know. She told me she hates the idea of me being with other people, and that she isn't seeing anyone besides me.

While I hadn't realized I would be getting into another relationship so soon, everything about being with Blair feels right. It doesn't feel rushed or like I am stepping in the wrong direction. If anything, I feel like I'm becoming the best version of myself that I've ever been. And it's all because of her.

"Okay, I didn't wanna tell you this because I was pretty positive I'd find some way to get out of doing it," I begin to say to Blair. We're holding hands and standing outside the rink, watching all of the skaters move around, some of them graceful, some of them making it look easy, and some of them falling on their asses. "But I've never actually done this before."

Blair's beautiful eyes stare back at me in wide surprise. But how could she be surprised?

"Do I really look like the type of person who does this kind of stuff?" I say in my defense.

She giggles. "Well, then… I'll just have to teach you!" Her eyes twinkle with amusement.

I smirk at her and brush my nose against hers affectionately. "I guess you will," I reply. "You better not let me fall, or I'm taking you down with me."

She giggles and takes my hand, and then drags me along to purchase the skate rentals. Then when we're all laced up and ready to go, we head over to the edge.

"Have you at least been rollerblading?" she asks.

"Well, yeah, of course. That's *much* more my style."

"Good, because it's similar to that. I'm sure you'll be fine."

I take her hand anyway, feeling deathly terrified as we step out onto the ice. It's so cold and hard… how do people not crack their heads open on it? The thought of it makes me shutter.

We don't even make it very far before I slip in my skates and tumble down. And just as promised, Blair falls with me. I hadn't even meant to do it, but I do weigh a lot more than her.

"Maybe—we should have—brought some protective gear," Blair says to me through her gasps of pain. I nod in agreement, and we get ourselves back to our feet. Then we look at each other and burst out laughing.

We spend the next half hour barely moving away from the edge of the rink as Blair continues to try to teach me. In my opinion, it's nothing like rollerblading. And I'm never going to get good at it. But it's cute how determined Blair is. She's like this with anything she does. It's refreshing that when she puts her mind to something, she achieves it. I never actually thought that was possible.

Later, I get to the point where we manage to somehow make it one entire lap around the ring without falling or gripping onto the walls. I probably could've gone even further, too, but the person standing on the edge of the rink outside makes me stop abruptly. Then Blair slams into my back as she skates behind me, and the two of us slide into the wall nearby, my eyes never leaving the person I'm seeing.

She is exactly the same as the last time I saw her.

Long dark hair. Piercing gaze. An unapproachable expression in her eyes. Her brows thick and dark, and her skin tan despite the cloudy and cold weather outside.

It's Jennifer.

"Dam?" Blair asks beside me. "Are you okay? Why did you stop?"

In front of me, Jennifer crosses her skinny little arms and puts her weight on one hip. Then, raising an eyebrow, she says, "Wow, Damascus. I didn't know you liked to ice skate." Her voice is judgmental and brutal. Heart-stoppingly, painstakingly brutal.

And damn, she's more beautiful than ever.

"Jennifer," is all I can manage to say, my lungs out of breath, but not from ice-skating. I'm too afraid to even look at the expression on Blair's face. She shouldn't have to see this.

Jennifer offers me a simple smile. One that doesn't reach her eyes. "It's good to see you. Been a while."

It seems as if all the pain she's caused me since she dumped me has come flooding back into my chest. I feel defenseless and heartbroken all over again.

There shouldn't be cheery happy Christmas music playing on the speakers around us right now. There should be a doom song playing. Like I'm about to battle a boss in a video game.

"Uh, yeah. It *has* been a while." I make sure not to say that it's good to see her, too, because it's definitely not. No matter how much my heart disagrees with me. I'm going to be strong and listen to my head and my stomach.

"Oh!" I take Blair's hand beside me and pull her

closer. "This is my girlfriend, Blair. Blair, this is my ex, Jennifer."

Jennifer's eyes widen for the briefest moment, but then she looks at Blair. "Nice to meet you," she says cordially.

I hope I am hurting her. I hope it physically causes her pain to know that I've already moved on. To know that I don't need her.

I can feel Blair tense up beside me. When I go to look at her, I noticed that her jaw is clenched, and she's glaring at my ex. She doesn't say anything to her.

"Well… we're gonna go now." I give Blair's hand a squeeze and gently pull her away from the wall so we can head over to the ice rink exit.

Later, when Jennifer is long gone, and Blair and I are heading to a coffee shop to get some hot chocolate, I can sense Blair's shifted mood. She's barely speaking to me.

I can't just pretend like what happened at the rink never happened. I might as well get it over with.

"I'm really sorry about what happened back there," I tell her. "I definitely hadn't expected that to be a place where I'd run into her."

I hold the door open to the small local coffee shop—not the one that Jennifer works at—and Blair steps inside, her eyes refusing to meet mine.

"It's fine."

I follow in after and race around so that I can be in front of her, then I grab both of her hands and peer down into her eyes. "I can tell it's not fine. Did I do something wrong?"

"I don't know, Dam. You just… you should've seen

your face… It was like I was witnessing love at first sight or something. You looked like a helpless puppy."

"No, I didn't."

The coffee shop is pretty busy, and Blair's voice isn't exactly quiet.

"Yes, you did, though. You had turned to complete mush. And it's okay; I completely understand why. I've never seen her before. But… she's gorgeous."

Suddenly, her eyes well with tears. Then she pulls her hands out of my grasp and goes back out the door into the cold.

Feeling horrible, I follow her.

"Blair! Where are you going?" I call to her as she walks across the street in the snow.

She doesn't answer me. So, I run to catch up. When I reach her side, she wipes her eyes quickly.

"Blair, talk to me." I hadn't meant to look at Jennifer any certain way. I was just surprised. She had to know that.

Blair stops walking, the two of us still in the middle of the street. "How am I supposed to compete with that?" she asks me. "I mean, seriously, Dam. Why didn't you tell me you were dating America's next top model?"

"Wait, I'm dating America's next top model?" I try to joke.

She doesn't find it funny. "I'm talking about Jennifer! I just don't know how you could possibly even compare us."

"Well, it's easy. I don't compare you. You're nothing like Jennifer."

"Oh, great, so you agree. I'm ugly."

I laugh at her pitifulness and pull her into a hug. She doesn't resist it, so I take it as a good sign.

"Blair, if you really don't think you're beautiful, you're insane. I will check you into a mental institution right now."

She looks up at me, so I wipe away the last tear still trailing down her cheek.

"I already never seem to compare to my sister. I hate that I feel like I'm never gonna be able to compare to your ex, either."

I look deep into her eyes. "Blair, if this isn't absolutely clear to you, I'm crazy about you. You might actually be the best thing that has ever happened to me. If you don't compare to Jennifer, it's because you are better, I swear."

My heart swells with happiness, and my stomach erupts with stupid butterflies as I speak. I realize, looking into Blair's teary eyes, that I one hundred percent mean it.

12

KENNETH

"So, I suppose you're going to be taking off soon to go visit your family for the holiday," Selena asks me. "Right?"

We're sitting on my sofa together, our thighs touching, I can't help but notice. *Home Alone* is playing on TV. Selena let me pick it.

I shrug. "I'm not really sure. What do you want to do?"

She tilts her head at me. "What do you mean?"

I feel heat creeping onto my face, embarrassed at my stupid mouth. I had sounded like I was asking her what she wanted to do, as if we were going to spend Christmas *together* or something. As if I wanted to do whatever *she* wanted to do.

"I mean… aren't you going to go home?"

Selena sighs like she's been waiting for this question. "Maybe. I just think there's a pretty good chance that Derek would assume I'm going there and show up."

From what I've gathered at work or at the stadium, Derek is still acting like he knows where Selena is. He is still acting like he wants her out of the public eye. After my boss' harrowing call yesterday, I had gone into work today hoping to get better information. Hoping to find some other way to get myself a story other than begging Selena to let me exploit her.

I even had a chance to talk to Derek today, if I wanted to. I saw him approaching me with an angry look on his face down by the locker room just before I left. The only reason I turned and walked the other way was because I was honestly afraid. I was worried that he was going to somehow get it out of me where Selena was. I was worried that I wouldn't be able to protect her.

"You have to face him at some point," I say to her.

Last night, after I made her cry, I gave her some time to cool down, then I went and softly knocked on her door. She cracked it open and apologized for breaking down. Then she said she was just terrified and needed more time to think it over. But I didn't have much more time to wait. So, I have to keep pressing.

She ignores my comment. "If you go, I'm more than

okay to stay here," she says. "I don't mind looking after the house. It could be kind of nice to spend a quiet Christmas by myself."

I look at her like she's crazy. "You want to be alone on Christmas?"

"Maybe? At least, I'd rather be alone than with Derek."

I get to my feet and pull my phone out of my pocket. Christmas is less than a week away, so if I'm going to make any plans, I need to do them soon.

"I'm going to go give my family a call. Figure out what the plan is. I'll be right back." I walk back into my bedroom and close my door, then I ring up my stepmom.

"Kenneth! So good to hear your voice," she says when she answers.

"Hey, so I want to come visit for Christmas," I tell her, not wasting any time. "I think we should discuss how we can make that happen."

13

———

BRENNAN

I don't answer the door when somebody knocks on it later the next day. All kinds of people have been coming over to try and talk to our family. Specifically, me.

I'm upstairs in the loft, using my parents' computer to do some paperwork for budgets at my job. So, I listen as Mom and Dad get up from their seats in the living room and go to answer it.

"What are you doing here?" I hear Mom ask. "You have some nerve."

This is the first thing I've heard them say to someone at the door that has piqued my interest. I lean over the banister and try to see who they're talking to, but they're blocking my view of the person.

"You have no right being on our property," Dad is saying to the mystery guest. I know it must be someone bad if even *Dad* is upset.

"Sorry, I-I just wanted to speak to… Brennan."

My stomach drops as I recognize the voice of the person speaking. Then I practically jump down the stairs, skipping every other step. I shove in between my parents and stand in front of our visitor. It's Leah.

"I got it, you guys," I tell my parents.

But they're mad at me, too. "Brennan, she shouldn't be here. And you shouldn't be talking to her."

I shoot Leah an apologetic glance before looking back at my parents. "Will you knock it off? It's not my problem that you two think Derek is a perfect little angel when he's not."

Then, before they can start yelling at me or bite out a mean reply, I step outside and join Leah in the cold and snowy air, closing the door behind me.

Leah runs a hand through her long brown hair. Her teeth are chattering from the cold. At least, I *think* from the cold.

"I-I am so sorry. I don't know why I came here. That was stupid of me."

I motion for us to step away from my front porch. It's better if we talk somewhere where cameramen aren't lingering nearby. As we begin walking, I realize I should've remembered my jacket.

"No, I'm glad you came," I tell her. "I'm sorry about my parents. Clearly, they're not on my side about the whole thing."

She nods her head, her hands in her pockets as we stroll down the sidewalk. The sun is about to finish setting, and we're walking in the direction of the last bits of its glow.

Leah doesn't immediately have a reply. There is definitely tension hanging in the air between us, words left unsaid, so I'm relieved when she finally speaks.

"I'm sorry for how I acted outside of Henderson's." She lets her hair fall in front of her. It strikes me as slightly odd because Leah was always such a confident, popular girl back in high school.

"Oh, yeah?" I ask her. "Why the change of heart?"

"I have the local news app on my phone. I saw a headline notification this morning about how you and your brother got into a fistfight outside of his house yesterday."

I wince. I should've paid more attention to the mysterious black car parked outside of the gate at Derek's place. I should have known that it was the paparazzi. But at the same time, I don't feel that bad about it—I'm glad that the world seems to know where I stand on the whole situation. I'm glad I'm doing what's right.

"Oh. That." I pull a hand out of the pocket of my jeans to inspect my scabbed-up knuckles. The cold air outside seems dangerous enough to split them back open.

Leah sneaks a look over at my hand as well. "You got him good," she says. "At least from what I could see in the picture, anyway."

"Thank you," I say awkwardly, my heart skipping a beat. Maybe I'm just glad to find out that she doesn't hate me after all.

"Yeah."

We turn the corner of my street and continue walking in silence for a little bit.

I wait as long as I can to see if she's going to say something else, but when I've had enough, I speak again. "So, uh, Leah," I start. "What else brings you to my house today? Was it just so you could apologize?"

Leah keeps her head down as we walk. I get the feeling that whatever she's about to tell me isn't something she likes to talk about.

"Um... I guess I just wanted to tell you that it's true."

The pitiful ham and cheese sandwich I had whipped up in the kitchen before heading to the computer upstairs after work revolts in my stomach.

"It's true?" I ask.

"Yes. About Derek. It wasn't me who made that anonymous post, and I still have yet to make one, but everything that all those other girls are saying. It's true. I-I know firsthand."

I stop walking, the news shaking me to my core. Derek had been abusive to her when they were together. Has he ever been good to *anyone*?

Leah doesn't stop walking with me, though. I get a feeling that maybe it's because it's easier for her to keep going than it is to stay still and have to look at me.

So, I jog a little to catch up to her, my entire body feeling like it's about to shut down from the cold outside. I really don't want to walk too much further without something warmer to wear.

"Are you okay?" I ask her, not really knowing what else to say.

She sighs and kicks a pile of frozen leaves into the snow. "I am now. It was a long time ago. But it definitely messed me up. He was a monster, Brennan. But he was so *liked* by everybody that no one else seemed to be able to see it. He had a way of making me feel powerless, like nobody would ever be on my side. So, I stayed silent. And I let it pretty much ruin me."

How the hell am I supposed to make up for that?

"I don't even really know what to say to you right now," I decide to tell her honestly. "If I'd had any idea…"

Finally, she sneaks a peek up at me. "It's not your fault. It's not my fault, either. It's no one but Derek's. Took me a long time to realize that. But thank you."

I offer her a small smile, then she looks away again.

"Besides, it's not all bad," she continues. "I run two support groups down at the town center, did you know that?"

"No, I didn't, actually."

Leah looks happy with herself. "When I figured out how to get my PTSD under control, if I even *do* have it under control, all I knew was that I wanted to help other people. I want to make sure that nobody feels the way I did. It may not always work, but there are generally a good amount of days where I feel like I've made an actual difference in people's lives."

I'm impressed. "That's amazing. Seriously, good for you."

To my astonishment, Leah gets a shadow of a smile across her face.

Derek may have messed her up, but from what I can tell about her, there's no way Leah is completely ruined, despite what she may think.

14

GISELLE

I imagine having a boyfriend is a lot more fun when you actually like boys.

Going out in public with Steve, holding his hand, and acting all lovey-dovey around him—it makes me want to run back inside and hurl into my toilet.

"I can't believe we're doing this!" Steve says happily beside me.

We're out and about in public, for the first time, letting the whole world see our relationship status. We are together. Steve is my boyfriend, and I am his girl-friend. Despite my previous rejection, somehow Steve still got a hold of me. And now, here I am.

I look up and give his face a fake smile, hating his stupid bright blonde hair, hating his stupid pretty blue eyes, and hating the way his eyebrows are so low on his forehead that they are nearly covering his eyes and making him look permanently pissed off.

Oh, and his ears stick out really far, too.

"Me, neither, *darling*," I say to him. Then I try really hard not to roll my eyes in case the paparazzi get a picture of it. I would hate for there to be a headline, "Trouble in Paradise? Giselle Cosgrove Seems to Want to Spend More Time with Eliza Leon than Her Own Boyfriend."

Because if that happens, I'm pretty sure I might die.

We are walking around the neighborhood outside of my apartment, one of the not-as-nice places around LA. My apartment building itself is nice; it's newly renovated and was one of the only locations where I could finan-cially afford the penthouse. But it isn't the best place for walking around.

Steve gives my hand a squeeze. "So, what are you doing for Christmas? Have you decided?"

"I'm going home," I say quickly, hoping he drops it.

"*We're* going home, you mean."

I shake my head at him. "Absolutely not, Steve. There's no way I'm taking you to meet my parents."

I told Eliza I was going to bring him home, but it was only to make her jealous! I don't actually want to!

Steve lets go of my hand and stops walking. My stomach dipping, I turn around to face him.

"I really want to make this work, Giselle," he tells me. "I know you want to make it work, too. Or else you wouldn't be here right now. Right?"

I chew the inside of my cheeks so hard that I think I might actually taste blood.

I look around to see if anybody can see us. But those who are around us don't seem to know who we are.

"I'll let them see that we're having a fight," Steve says to me. "I'll even give an interview *personally*."

I walk back over to him and throw my arms around his neck, my heart racing. Then I give him a hug and kiss him on the cheek. "Okay, okay. Of course, you can come home with me for Christmas."

He resumes holding my hand and walking down the street with me. Just like that, he's back to smiling happily like he's the luckiest guy in the world. He keeps shooting me wide eyes like he's in love with me or something. It will make for great photos.

"I'm hungry," he says. Then he points at a taco stand just across the street. "Tacos sound good?"

"Steve, you silly man! Don't you remember that I am a model? I can't have sketchy tacos from a sketchy stand on the street corner." I keep a smile on my face, even though it's strained. They say it takes many more muscles to frown than to smile, but I beg to differ. My face legitimately hurts from keeping this up.

"Fine. Then you can sit with me while I have some tacos," Steve replies.

We cross the street and walk over to the stand, then a

teenage girl recognizes me with her boyfriend and squeals. She quickly whips out a magazine from her bag and goes to a page with me on it. "Oh my gosh! I'm so sorry, but will you please sign this?" she asks me.

I grin at her. "I'd be happy to!"

Anything other than sitting here watching Steve stuff his face full of mystery meat. I take the girl's magazine and swirl out my signature with her black sharpie. Then she asks for a photo, and I put my arm around her as her boyfriend takes a picture.

"You are literally such an inspiration!" the girl says to me. "I can't believe I actually got to meet you!"

I put a hand to my heart. "Oh, that is so freaking sweet!" I say back. I sort of wish this random fan would stay here and keep chatting with me, but she would never think that I'd *want* to do that, so she gives me a shy wave, and her and her boyfriend resume walking past.

I sigh and turn back to Steve. Sometimes being famous isn't all it's cracked up to be.

15

———

DAMASCUS

elieve me, the last thing I wanted was for the Jennifer sighting yesterday to stir something bad up inside of me. And I know it's a lame excuse, but I am being honest when I say this—I can't help it.

And what puts me in an even *worse* mood today is the fact that the one person I want to talk to about how I'm feeling isn't around for me to do so. I just think it's unfair. I think the entire world is unfair.

During the time I've spent dating Blair, she has

gotten to learn a little bit about my bad side. About the darkness inside of me. About my rebellious urges. But still, she has no idea what makes me the way I am. She knows nothing about my past, nothing except about Jennifer.

When Blair tries to text and call me today, it's not that I don't want to talk to her. It's not that I don't like her anymore. It's not that I've forgotten that I know how good she is for me. She just doesn't need to see me like this. She doesn't need to be the one to talk me down from my ledge. It's not fair to her.

Before me, she was living this perfect, quaint, simple, happy life, and then I bulldozed my way in, this dark shadow sucking her in. I don't really know how to explain it, but I have this constant dread inside me of what mine and Blair's future holds. I'm going to turn her into me. While she changes me for the better, I'm going to change her for the worse. And knowing this, why the hell am I being so selfish and continuing to stay with her?

I park my truck a few blocks away from the protesters. I'm looking forward to stirring up some mayhem. There's no better way to distract myself than by giving others what they deserve.

It's still early enough in the day that I know the protesters will still be on the street corner with their ridiculous signs and posters, making women feel terrible about themselves. Don't these idiots know that there isn't only one reason to go into this family planning institution?

I grab the only item I need today out of the backseat

and carry it discreetly inside my unzipped black jacket as I stroll along the sidewalk. I grin at the sight of the protesters on the corner. I know what I'm about to do could get me easily arrested, but I just don't care. I don't care what happens to me. The world is unfair, and it'll probably keep being unfair. This is just my one little way to get back at it.

By the time they all see me coming, I stop walking only a few feet away from them.

"It's just not right!" one woman says to me, a sign in her hand depicting something horrible that I absolutely don't agree with.

I can tell they're waiting to see if I'm here to join them or if I'm against them.

I roll my eyes and pull out the item I brought with me. I open the carton of eggs and pick one up, and I chuck it at the first lady who spoke. It bursts open on her pretty white blouse, covering her in goop.

There are four people here today, three of them women and one of them a man. I can easily dodge them as they come at me, yelling and cursing. I continue to pick eggs up from my carton and chuck it at them. I hit their signs. I hit their chests. I hit their butts. I even managed to clock the guy right in between the eyes. All the while, I am laughing hysterically.

Yeah, this is *just* what I needed.

As I had been anticipating, I did end up getting arrested. A cop pulled up just shortly after the four of them were able to wrestle me into a tight hold, only after the man punched me hard enough in the cheek to make me fall over. I hadn't anticipated him being *actually* strong.

Luckily, the cop who puts me in the backseat of his car has become somewhat of a friend of mine over the years. He is an older dude, in his sixties, with a big belly from eating too much pizza and drinking too much beer, and he has a perfectly cul-de-sac-shaped head of hair.

"I gotta take you back to the station, and someone's got to come to pick you up."

"Oh, come on, Carl," I complain in the backseat. "I'm not even drunk."

"Damascus, don't make me breathalyze you."

I grumble and lean back into my seat. Already, I know I'm in trouble. Because there's only one person I can call. It's not Andrew. He left a couple days ago to head home for the holiday.

So, when we get back to the station, I give the number a call, and then I wait on the chair next to Carl's desk in shame.

When Blair walks into the station and meets my eyes, I can clearly see the disappointment in hers.

"Wait, that doesn't look like Jennifer," Carl comments. Luckily, Blair is too far away for her to hear it.

"No, it sure isn't." I pick up my jacket and throw it over my shoulder, then I leave Carl's desk and head over to my girlfriend, who is standing uncomfortably by the door.

"Well, this is the first time I've ever had to do this," she tells me.

"Oh, come on. It's not like I was arrested. He just had to pick me up."

She shoots me a dirty look and walks out front. I can't help but think of how Jennifer would've reacted if she had been the one to pick me up, if she were still my girlfriend. She would've made out with me intensely in front of the entire staff of officers, then she would've jumped on my back and had me carry her out the front door. She would've whispered in my ear or something like, "Hell, yeah, baby," and she would've been happy that I took a stand.

Blair couldn't be more the opposite.

I follow her outside and drag myself slowly behind, and she looks over her shoulder to see why I'm not catching up with her.

I had already explained to her over the phone what I had done, and why I got picked up by Carl, because she told me she refused to come get me until I did.

"What's going on with you?" she asks, slowing her pace so she can walk beside me.

"What do you mean?"

"I *mean*, you can't just go around egging people! What the hell is wrong with you?"

"Do you think the girls going into that clinic wanted to be guilt-tripped beforehand? Do you think they deserved it?"

She looks offended. "Of course not! It's not like I'm on the protesters' side!"

"Good, then there is no problem between us, and no reason for you to be mad at me right now."

We reach her car, a cute little Trailblazer that apparently does well in the snow, but she doesn't move to get inside of it. Instead, she leans against her trunk, crosses her arms, and stares at me.

"What?" I ask, not looking at her. I tilt my head back all the way up to the sky so she can see how annoyed I am. "Can I please just go home?" I feel slightly like I'm begging my mother right now.

"Are you drunk?"

This pisses me off. "No, I'm not. Thanks for thinking so."

"Look, I don't know what's going on with you, or why you did that, and I don't expect you to tell me, either. But I just…"

"You're so much better than me. You're too… good for me," I tell her. "Did you know that?"

"No, but I'm starting to," she replies, still looking like she's really mad at me for some reason.

Good. I'm glad she's standing her ground. I'm glad she doesn't want to be anything like me.

She sighs and steps away from her car. "I didn't mean that. I just know you can be so much better. I know that *you* know you're better than this. There are other ways to get back at people than doing things that are going to get you in trouble."

"We can't all be like you, Blair."

She glowers at me. "Don't do that, Damascus."

I turn away from her.

She continues. "Don't try to make me feel bad for

the way that I live my life just because you don't like the way that you live yours."

Her words cut me deeper than I expected them to.

I react before thinking. "You know what, screw this. I don't need a ride," I say to her. Then I do what I do best.

I run.

I'M SO pissed at Blair that I decide I'm going to go to an ugly sweater party. Without her. We had mentioned going together, but I didn't talk to her the rest of the day, and she didn't try to reach out to me, either. So, solo it is.

I'm not really the kind of guy who owns an ugly sweater, so I dig through Andy's closet to see what I can find. Go figure—he has one covered with cats playing with yarn balls.

I put it on, but then I put on a plain black sweater over it to see if maybe I can get away with it.

The large parties in Quincy are usually thrown at The Warehouse. It's this abandoned place out in a grassy field, where people have hung out so often that it actually doesn't seem too abandoned anymore. There's even a good chance that somebody bought it and converted it into a place just to throw parties, but I don't know. I don't throw the parties; I just show up at them.

I also make sure I am nicely intoxicated before I go inside. I had to run back to my truck after the fight with Blair, and I drove it straight to the grocery store and grabbed myself a bottle of Jack Daniels. Now I am sitting in the front seat of my truck, sipping it straight from the bottle.

Part of me hopes that Blair is inside with her friends, but a bigger part of me has a feeling she won't be. Not a lot of college-goers know about this place; it seems to be specifically reserved for the locals.

I eventually get out of my truck and head to the entrance, where I am greeted by a bouncer. I'm pretty sure he works at the gas station down the street usually.

"Can't come in without a sweater," he says to me. Then he points to the sign next to him hanging on the wall. It does indeed say that an ugly sweater is required for entry. So, I groan and rip off my black sweater to reveal the cat one underneath.

He grunts in a half-laugh at me, then lets me inside. Everything is red and green. String lights are hung everywhere, as well as disco balls and strobe lights. The Warehouse is two stories, all the dancing happening on the bottom floor, where the DJ is set up, while the people upstairs hang out and talk with each other.

And fine, since this is a *local* party, maybe there *is* somebody else I'm hoping will be here.

I don't know what it is, but ever since I saw Jennifer yesterday, I can't get her out of my head.

But the drunker I get, the more I feel like maybe it's for the best that I find Jennifer. I feel like Blair is going to dump me anyway. Why would she want to be with a guy like me? I might as well try to get Jennifer back now.

I walk around the entire party, saying hi to some people whom I hang out with sometimes, and stopping at the bar frequently for red and green Jell-O shots and more whiskey. I even walk onto the dance floor, though I don't do any dancing. I'm just checking out everyone who's here.

Go figure, the dance floor is where somebody taps me on the shoulder, and I turn around to see Jennifer. She loves to dance. Maybe that's why I came onto the dancefloor in the first place.

"I like your sweater," she says to me. *Her* sweater is more the Freddy Krueger type. It has green and red stripes with a couple holes poked into it. It's so completely Jennifer.

"What are you doing here?" I slur.

She raises her eyebrows. "*Someone's* drunk," she notices.

"What gave you that idea?"

"You're on a dance floor, for one."

"Are you asking me to dance?" I joke. "Cuz I'm not really into that kind of thing, but we can go somewhere and talk if you want."

She rolls her eyes at me, but then she takes my hand and pulls me along. It feels weird having my hand in hers again. It's literally been months. And I had just gotten used to having Blair's hand in mine, instead. Blair's hand is a little smaller, and she holds mine much tighter than Jennifer does, like she doesn't want to let me go.

Jennifer leads me up the stairs so we can have a quieter place to talk. God only knows what she is going to say to me right now.

"So, I will just get right to it," she starts. We sit down

on some cold folding chairs, our knees touching each other. "I was really surprised to see you with another girl yesterday."

"Oh, I'm sorry, did you expect me to be crying over you much longer than this?"

She looks embarrassed. "You barely even tried to talk to me after we ended things."

"You dumped me, Jennifer. Why would I want to talk to you?"

Jennifer frowns. "I know, but still. We were together for a while. I thought you would at least try. Instead, I see you at the skating rink—somewhere I *never* thought I'd catch you, by the way—and you're with some preppy girl having the time of your life. I don't know… It sucked."

"Welcome to my world," I think I say to myself.

Turns out, I said it out loud.

16

———

KENNETH

The more I think about it, the more it seems to make sense just to invite Selena to spend Christmas with me. I can't stand the thought of her hanging out here in my house alone. Especially with nobody around to protect her from Derek, should he somehow figure out where she is.

I don't know why, though. I'm nervous to ask her. It would be just as friends anyway, so I shouldn't be so scared of getting rejected.

The thought comes to me while I'm getting ready for work one morning, and I can hear Selena out in the kitchen making herself her usual breakfast—two egg whites on a piece of whole-grain toast. She likes to use that everything-bagel seasoning stuff. She made me buy some, and now I love it, too.

As soon as I finish styling my hair in the mirror, I double-check that I look okay, then I head out of the bathroom and walk into the kitchen. Selena is barefoot, wearing pink PJ shorts and a gray cropped sweater.

"Good morning," I say to her, feeling weird and formal for some reason.

She turns around and smiles at me, and my stomach dips.

"Good morning!" she says back. She has her plate of breakfast in one hand and a glass of orange juice in the other. "Breakfast?"

She asks me this every morning. I never have breakfast. I like to sleep in for as long as possible and then rush out the door, grab myself some gas station coffee, and get the job done.

I shake my head at her and smile. Then I run a hand through my hair because of the nerves, but *then* I'm worried I've messed up my hair, and that I'm going to have to go back to the bathroom to check it before I leave.

"You look stressed out," she notices. She notices a lot of things about me. Either we've just gotten to know each other pretty well already, or she's good at reading people.

I shrug. "So, I have an idea," I start before I chicken out.

She tilts her head at me and goes to sit at the table. I walk over to it and pick up all my belongings to take to work.

"And what would that be?" she asks. I can tell that she's worried it's going to be Derek-related. At least she'll be happy to hear that it's not.

"I think you should spend Christmas with me," I say. I finally let out the long breath I realize I've been holding in. *There, I did it.*

She purses her lips and looks away, her eyes in thought. "In … LA?"

"Yeah. Um, I just think it's better than you being here alone. It would be as friends, of course."

She hasn't even touched her breakfast yet. "Why do you want me to come with you?" Her voice is soft, and the way she's looking at me is making my stomach squirm uncomfortably.

I itch the back of my neck. "I just told you, ya goof."

She smirks at me. "That's … Wow."

I point at her plate. "You should eat. Before it gets cold. You can think it over; it was just a thought."

She still doesn't touch it. We are silent for a bit.

"Alright, if you're not gonna touch it, then give *me* the plate, and I'll eat it."

I'm only joking, and she knows this, so she chuckles. "I guess I really don't want to go home to my parents. And the thought of being here all alone is kind of sad and pitiful, isn't it?"

Hope rises in me. "Exactly!"

She shrugs, and then finally takes a bite of her toast. Then with a mouth full of food, she replies. "Alright, I'm in."

17

GISELLE

"I literally thought places like this only existed in movies and books," Steve says to me as we step off the plane and enter the airport of my hometown.

I shrug at him and walk ahead. I want to talk to Steve as little as possible.

He's quick to catch up to me and hold my hand. As we walk, a few people stop and take pictures of me, but thankfully, none of them are trying to approach. Especially since I don't have Lonnie or Bryan with me. I don't think I would be happy knowing that I took them away from their Christmas.

Steve squeezes my hand as we walk, both of us dragging one suitcase behind us. "You gotta talk to me at some point," he says.

"I *am* talking to you."

I am also sick to my stomach because I'm worried I'm going to do something that upsets him. It would be so easy for him to use my family against me.

"Yeah, but I don't think—"

"Steve?!"

We both snap our heads up, and I have to admit that I'm totally confused. How in the hell does somebody at the Quincy airport know who *Steve* is? He's not the one who used to live here.

Steve grins wide when he notices an attractive man walking in our direction with a smile on his face, too. Behind him is a tiny woman, wearing a jacket with the hood on and sunglasses like she doesn't want to be recognized.

The two men hug as the woman and I stand here awkwardly.

"What the hell are you doing here, man?" the guy asks my boyfriend.

"Spending Christmas with my girl's family!" Steve says.

His friend looks at me, then his eyes widen. "Giselle Cosgrove?"

"Um, hello," I say.

"Wow, I can't believe it actually happened!" he says,

holding out his hand. "So good to meet you! Steve talks about you nonstop. You are like, his *dream* girl. I'm Kenneth."

I take his hand and shake it. Then I plaster on that fake smile that I've gotten so good at lately. "That's sweet. Nice to meet you, too."

"What are *you* doing here?" Steve asks Kenneth. The woman behind him is still saying nothing and looks like she would rather be anywhere else. It looks as if she is in a similar situation as me. *But what do I know?*

"Dude, I told you, I have work here. For now," Kenneth explains. "But I'm headed home for the holiday, with my friend here, Alexis."

Alexis nods her head at us and raises a hand in hello, but doesn't speak.

I wave back at her. "Hello," I say.

Steve gives her a big smile, then looks back at his friend. "Well, it's kinda like we're trading places, then," he jokes.

"*Kenny*," the girl warns.

Kenneth winces. "Well, have fun here. It's cold as hell, and there's nothing to do! No offense, Giselle. I grew up here, too."

"We both left for a reason," I say. Now that I look closer at him, he does look a little bit familiar. I think he might have graduated from Quincy High the year before I started.

"We have to go catch our flight. It was good seeing you guys. Merry Christmas."

"Merry Christmas!"

The two take off, heading to their gate, the girl keeping her head down and walking close to Kenny.

Steve goes back to taking my hand and leading us toward our rental car place. "Huh," he says. "Small world."

18

DAMASCUS

I feel pretty lousy sitting here in the support group today. Not only because I acted like a jackass the last time I was here, but because of the girl problems I am dealing with, too.

I just don't get it. Things were going amazing with Blair. She was helping me get over Jennifer. But now *Blair* is mad at me.

Blair is currently mad at me, and Jennifer has recently admitted that she misses me. And now my head is all confused and messed up again, and my heart hurts. Especially since it's Christmas Eve, and I already hate this time of year as it is.

Thankfully, the support group leader knows me well enough now to help me calm down. The entire meeting, she doesn't make me speak, and she hardly even looks at me or pretends to know I'm here, so I'm able to just sit in silence and listen.

At the end of the session, as everyone is heading out the door, the support group leader calls out to me, wanting me to hang back.

I turn around, only steps away from the exit door.

"I'm supposed to give Shawn a call," she says to me. "I was wondering if you wanted to say hi."

Finally, some good news.

I can't help but smile at her a little. "Yeah, I would love that. Thanks."

She motions for me to sit down in the metal chair next to her. Then she gets on her smartphone and calls Shawn. He answers quickly, sitting in a comfy chair and looking happy. I can tell that whatever he's using to video chat us is propped up against something so that he doesn't have to try and use his hands.

"Leah!" Shawn greets, beaming at the support group leader.

Leah grins back at him. "It's not just me. Somebody else wants to say hi to you, too!"

She moves the camera so that I am on the screen, and Shawn smiles at me. "Damascus?!"

It gives me a pit in my stomach to see and hear how much his ALS has progressed. His voice is a lot more slurred than I remember, and I can tell just by looking at his torso how his muscles have started weakening. Instantly, I feel the lump in my throat.

But I smile at the man anyway. "Hey, Shawn. Merry Christmas."

He nods his head. "How are you holding up?"

"I guess I could be worse," I say with a sly smile. It's a joke we always use with each other. He thinks it's funny when I complain about my crappy life, and then look at him and say, "But at least I'm not you." It's slightly morbid, but we think that's what makes it funny. And ironic, too, because sometimes I actually do wish I were him.

Shawn and I used to attend these ALS support meetings together back when he lived here in town. Leah has been our group leader the entire time. For some reason, out of everyone who came and went, the three of us have built a relationship that stuck.

"We sure do miss having you here," Leah says to Shawn.

"Is it crazy for me to admit that I sort of miss it, too?" he asks. Leah and I both chuckle.

"Well, you should come back sometime," Leah suggests.

"Yeah! Come see us. I bet this place is *way* cooler than your fancy new mansion out there in LA," I join in.

Shawn laughs, then the three of us stay and talk a lot longer than I expected.

When Shawn has to go to a doctor's appointment, Leah hangs up. I help her collect and carry her things, then we walk outside of the building together. We had another snowfall last night and this morning, so fresh snow goes up to our ankles as we walk down the steps and onto the sidewalk. The two of us are cracking up, our shoulders bumping into each other, over the dumb, rich-person-thing that Shawn had been complaining about when we were on the phone with him.

I'm grateful to have Shawn and Leah this Christmas season; they seem to be the only two consistent people in my life.

We begin to cross the street, but then Leah jumps, startled by something. I stop walking and look at her, noticing that she had abruptly stopped laughing and is now staring at something across from us.

I look up and see that just across the street on the snow-covered sidewalk, Jennifer is standing there, tears in her eyes as she points a finger at me.

"Jennifer?" I ask. Next to me, Leah stands frozen.

"See, Damascus?" Jennifer asks in a shaky voice that steadily grows louder. "This. This is the reason I *dumped* you!"

I look behind me… at the sign outside the entrance to the building. The sign that reads, *Support Group Meeting Today!*

Then I turn back to Jennifer incredulously. There was a reason I never told her that I was going to therapy.

I take a few angry steps toward her, away from Leah. "Wait, *what?*" I ask, my pulse rising.

"I knew I made the right choice!" Jennifer shouts back. "When I saw you at the ugly sweater party, I should have walked the other way!"

"What the hell is the matter with you?!" I shout. I don't think I've ever felt angrier at her. Not even when she first dumped me. I had always been afraid that I might get this reaction if I told someone close to me about my therapy sessions. I had been right to close myself off. People are cruel.

Jennifer looks like she's about to reply to me, probably to say more offensive, hurtful things, but then a voice yelling from a car at a stop sign to the north of us makes us both turn our heads.

Blair is sticking her head out of the passenger window of her family's vehicle, a crushed expression on her face. "Damascus?!" she calls. Then the car resumes driving, and Blair and I make eye contact until I can't see her anymore.

Great. It's the day of Christmas Eve, and my girlfriend has just caught me in the snow with my ex.

19

BRENNAN

This is a new one for me.

It's Christmas Eve, and I'm sitting by myself at the bar inside of Henderson's. Normally, I'd be at my house or at Brielle's parents' house, hanging out with our families, sitting by warm fires, and stuffing our faces. Normally, I'd get to see Derek, and the two of us would hang out, joke around with each other, and make Mom mad together accidentally.

It amazes me how quickly things can change.

Mom and Dad are still furious at me for fighting Derek. They won't talk to me, nor will they even look at me.

Part of me feels like they know that the rumors about my brother are true, but they're sticking by their son because they feel like it's their job. Because they feel like they can somehow make this all go away. I'm pretty sure Mom would be devastated to have everyone in Quincy think she raised a wife beater.

The door to the bar opens, and large, loud voices suddenly fill the air. When I look up, I see a group of people of all ages. White-haired men, middle-aged women, and some people who barely even look old enough to drink. Amongst them, is Leah.

"Jane!" a large, old guy cries to the bartender.

Jane beams at them. "I was wondering what time I'd see you all tonight!" She heads around the bar and goes over to start writing down everyone's drink order.

After Leah tells Jane what she wants, she starts heading my way with a smile on her face. "I can't say I've ever seen you here on Christmas Eve," she comments. She and the people she's with are bundled up in warm coats, hats, scarves, and mittens, and none of them make any move to take any of the layers off.

I shrug, feeling sorry for myself but not really caring for her to notice. "I might be starting a new Christmas Eve tradition," I say. "I am still testing it out."

She looks around herself. "Are you meeting anyone?"

I shake my head at her. "Just me tonight."

She doesn't look satisfied. "On Christmas Eve?"

I nod at her. *Thanks for rubbing it in.*

"Well, that just won't do," she says with a frown.

Jane walks around behind the bar to start making all of their drinks. When she sees Leah and me together, something seems to click in her brain. "Is this who you were waiting for all day last week?" she asks me, mixing something in a metal shaker.

Heat creeps into my face. "Yeah, but not for the reason you're probably thinking."

"Are you going on their bar crawl with them?" Jane asks.

"Bar crawl?" I look back and forth between the two of them.

"I was just about to ask him, Jane," Leah explains. Then she smiles at me. "We have a Christmas Eve bar crawl every year. It's my family's tradition. After dinner, we hit as many bars as we can before midnight—those of us who don't have little ones anyway."

"That sounds amazing!" I tell her, feeling incredibly jealous. Going on a bar crawl with my family would be a blast. It would be hilarious to see Mom drunk. It's something she rarely does.

Leah perks up a bit. "Good," she says. "Then you are coming with us!"

I look over at her family. They all look excited, some of them maybe already buzzed. About twelve people are doing the crawl, so maybe they won't even notice if I tag along.

"Are you sure?" I ask, not wanting to impose. But I *do* want to go.

She grabs my shoulders and shakes them excitedly.

This Leah seems a lot bubblier and more fun than the Leah I talked to outside my house.

"Yes, I'm sure!" she cries. "You have to drink that fast, because we only stay at each place a little bit!" She picks up my beer and puts it in my hand.

I laugh and began drinking the rest of it.

They may not be *my* family, but at least I'll be getting some family time this Christmas.

20

KENNETH

As I pull onto the street of my father's house, I drum my fingers on the steering wheel of my car.

"Oh my gosh…" Selena breathes, staring out the window. "Where does your family *live*?"

"We're on his street!" I explain with a smile. At least I think we are. I haven't been to my dad's new house yet, but I was given directions from my stepmom.

"Is your dad like, famous or something?" Selena

asks, still not turning to look back at me. She's too mesmerized by the massive houses we are passing.

"Um, something like that." I should probably just get it over with and tell her the truth. "So, I need to talk to you about something."

This gets her to finally turn around and look at me. Her eyes immediately fill with concern. "What is it? Did you not tell them I was coming?"

I cringe a little. "Well … I sort of didn't tell my dad that *either* of us was coming."

Selena purses her lips and closes her eyes.

I approach the gate in front of my father and my stepmom's house. My stepmom must've been waiting for me to get here because before I can even unroll my window to use the call box, the gate begins to open.

I continue explaining myself to Selena. "My dad —I don't really like to talk about it much, but he's… sick. He has ALS. I guess it's progressing pretty quickly these days, but every time I try to see him, he shoots me down. He doesn't even want to talk to me."

"Oh, gosh," Selena says, putting a hand over her mouth.

I park the car in the circular driveway, and some random man comes and helps us out. Selena looks flustered as her door opens, and the man holds his hand out to her, but she gets out of the car, trying not to break eye contact with me.

I get out of the car as well.

"I can go move your vehicle into the garage, if you'd like," the man says to me.

"No, we're fine, thank you. Uh … We just need a minute, if that's okay."

"Certainly," the man says, turning and heading back inside the incredible house.

Selena doesn't even seem interested in looking at how grand my dad's new place is, even though she had been mesmerized by the other houses on the drive over. Right now, she is only focused on me. "I am… I'm so *sorry*, for one," she begins, taking a step closer to me. "And two,"—she hits me on the arm—"how could you not warn me about this ahead of time?!"

I laugh as she shows her embarrassment.

"I didn't know we weren't invited, I didn't know your dad is sick, *and* I didn't know your family is filthy rich and famous!" she cries. "If I had, I would've maybe thought harder about my outfit!"

I roll my eyes at her. "You look beautiful."

I don't mean for the compliment to sound flirty, but it's just the truth. She's wearing a simple, cream cashmere sweater and black jeans. Her makeup is soft and light, and her blonde bob looks silky and straight.

I see movement behind her, and I look up to find my stepmom, Eliza, hurrying down the steps with an excited smile on her face. She waves at me frantically. "Kenny! I'm so happy to see you! Merry Christmas!"

Selena turns around to see who is speaking, and her jaw drops. I feel a little bit bad about not telling her who my stepmom is ahead of time.

I hug Eliza warmly, and she squeezes my shoulders when we break apart.

"You look wonderful," she tells me. I can tell she is

shocked to see Selena next to me. I've never brought a girl home. Ever. "And who is *this*?"

"This is my friend, Selena," I say. "And I mean it when I say *friend*, too." I can't have her getting ideas and making things uncomfortable for Selena.

To my surprise, Eliza gives Selena a hug. Selena hugs her back, her eyes meeting mine as I watch her mouth, "Oh my gosh," to me. I chuckle.

"Any friend of Kenneth's is a friend of mine," Eliza says. "I'm sure as soon as Shawn sees you, he'll forget why he's been pushing you away in the first place." She motions for us to follow her inside.

"It's wonderful to meet you, Mrs. Leon," Selena says as we walk.

"Please, *Eliza* is fine."

We go inside their new waterfront mansion, and Selena and I wait in the foyer while Eliza goes to get my father. My heart is pounding with the anticipation of seeing him. We used to be really close when I was a kid, but we started to butt heads a lot when I was a teenager. He tried to have strict rules with me, and I thoroughly enjoyed breaking them. Even when we both moved to LA, we only saw each other over the holidays. But then when he got his ALS, he started not wanting to see me at all.

Well, I'm here now, hoping to change that.

I'm surprised when my dad finally comes around the corner. He is not using a walker or a cane. He standing on his own two feet.

And he doesn't look happy to see me.

21

GISELLE

*I*t's weird waking up in my old bedroom, but I guess I appreciate the fact that my parents didn't convert it into something else. I'm pretty sure they'll probably end up keeping it like this until I'm retired. They always want me to feel like I have somewhere to come home to, should things not work out for me in LA.

I know it's Christmas day, but it's still remarkably early, so I take some time going through some of my drawers and looking around in my closet. I love the nostalgic feeling of going through all of my old belongings. I even find a journal of mine from when I was in high school. When I read through the entries, I smile. If only my fifteen-year-old self had known what her future had in store.

A man's voice coming from downstairs that doesn't sound like my father's catches my attention, so I walk out of my bedroom and head over to the railing. Peering down into the kitchen, I see that Steve—who normally prefers to sleep in and hates mornings—is already awake, talking with my family over coffee. And here I was thinking I probably woke up first.

Who starts their Christmas morning before six? I guess the Cosgrove family does.

I put on my Christmas slippers and robe, hoping my sister has on the matching set that I bought for her, too. Then I go downstairs and join everyone.

"Merry Christmas!" they yell at me.

"Merry Christmas," I say with a tired smile. Steve walks over and kisses my cheek. I give him a quick hug so that my family will buy it. Steve had slept in the guest room last night. We haven't exactly ever slept in the same bed before, and Christmas Eve in my old high school bedroom didn't seem like the best place to start.

"Steve is telling us more about how you two met," my short, little mother tells me. I didn't get my height from her; she's a little five-foot-two woman with wide hips and permed red hair. "How some famous fashion designer introduced you."

My stomach dips at the thought of Eliza. I wonder

what she's up to on this lovely Christmas morning. Outside my window, it's snowing, but I bet in LA, it's sunny and bright.

"That's… lovely," I say to Mom. Then I wiggle my eyebrows at my little sister. "Love your robe and slippers." We're pretty much matching, except for the fact that hers have green and red stripes, and mine have red and white stripes.

Blair hugs her robe tighter to herself. "Thanks!" she says with a smile.

But if I know my sister well enough, I can tell she's in a bad mood. She might be smiling, but there had been something about her tone that told me she's not feeling the Christmas spirit.

"What's going on with you, B?" I ask. I'm only going to get to spend so much time with her this trip, so I have to make the most of it. I love my little sister more than anything.

Blair shrugs. "When Dad and I were coming back from the store yesterday morning, I saw Damascus hanging out in the town square with his ex. The one who really messed him up."

I cringe. Blair has talked to me nonstop about her new boyfriend on the phone, but the way she makes it sound, Damascus seems like a moody, depressed, bad boy. I didn't think that was Blair's type.

"That's horrible," I say. "Did you find out why they were together?"

Blair shakes her head and yawns. I wonder if she even got any sleep last night. "No. I haven't exactly talked to him yet. I was already mad at him for something else, and now it seems like a bunch of little things are starting to pile up."

"We haven't even gotten to meet him yet," Dad informs me. At nearly seven feet, my dad towers over pretty much everybody we meet. He's the person I get my model-esque figure from. Poor Blair got the short end of the stick. Literally.

"No?" I ask.

Blair shrugs again. "I was going to have him come over today, but now I don't think I want to see him."

"Are you sure?"

"I don't want to let him ruin my Christmas. Or my time with you," she says. Then she grins at me and changes the subject. "So, now can we start opening presents?"

WE'RE MORE than halfway through getting everything opened, and I'm loving every second of watching my sister and my parents open the incredible gifts I had mailed to the house before coming. I love the fact that I can afford to buy them pretty much whatever they want. It's way more exciting than anything *they* could give *me*. I spoiled my family this year with the newest electronic gadgets, then I gave Blair tickets to a music festival, and I bought my parents a cruise. They were so excited that they jumped up and down and smothered me in hugs.

"I'm going to feel like such an old lady on a cruise ship!" Mom cries as Blair goes to unwrap another gift.

My mother is definitely not one to fit the fifty-year-old woman stereotype, but she has always wanted to go on a cruise.

Somebody knocks on the front door, and all of us stop opening gifts and look over at it.

"If that is who I think it is, I'm not speaking to him," Blair snaps. I eagerly get to my feet. I'm very curious to meet Blair's new boyfriend.

22

BRENNAN

"**W**hat the hell?!"

I snap my eyes open. For a moment, I forget where I am. All I know is that I apparently slept on the floor.

"Get out of my house!"

Confused and barely awake, I raise my head and see Leah curled up in a ball on the yellow sofa that I'm lying in front of. Then I realize we are inside her house, and it is *her* who is yelling at *me*.

"I'm serious, Brennan! Get out!" she shouts.

I quickly sit myself up and grab my t-shirt off the floor. Then I throw it over my head as I get to my feet, and she gets to hers, too.

She's furious, for some reason, still wearing the outfit she wore last night, her hair a brown, tangled mess. Right now, she looks a little bit like she's about to take a swing at me.

"Leah?" I try, suddenly on high alert. "What's wrong?"

"What's *wrong*?!" she repeats, clutching her hair and tugging it. "You're in my *house*! You're shirtless and sleeping in my house!"

"Okay?"

She steps away from me. "I—last night! How did this even happen? I don't remember anything!"

I reach my hands out like I'm trying to tame a feral animal. I just want to calm her down. "Leah, it's okay."

She picks a pillow up from her sofa and chucks it at me. "I'm serious, Brennan, you need to get out of here right now!"

I catch it in my hands and give her a stunned look. "What's going on? Why are you mad?"

I can't recall ever being woken up like this on Christmas before.

"Brennan!" she screams. Then she turns away from me and hugs herself.

Not wanting to piss her off any further, I grab my coat and shoes, and walk out her front door.

I have absolutely no idea what just happened.

23

KENNETH

$\mathcal{A}$s I'm furiously driving away from my father's house, Selena gently grabs my forearm. "Kenneth, please just pull over."

"Why?" I snap at her. Looking around us, there's nothing but big leafy trees.

"Because you shouldn't drive when you're upset like this. You could get us both killed."

Those words make me stop and think for a moment.

I don't want to make Selena afraid—as angry as I am at my family right now—so I pull over to the side and put my car in park.

I heave deep, angry breaths, not wanting to look at Selena. I am embarrassed and ashamed. Not to mention hurt. Not to mention completely wrecked over the fact that my father is dying and doesn't want me around him.

"Thank you," Selena says. Then she unbuckles her seatbelt and opens the car door.

"What are you doing?" I ask.

"Come on," she says to me. She steps out of the car and starts walking into the trees.

"Damn it," I mutter. Then I get out of the car and go to follow her, even though I don't exactly want to be around her right now. I don't want to be around *anyone*. But seeing as I'm the one who had this genius plan in the first place, I can't just tell Selena to leave me alone.

Back at my dad's new place, he had taken one look at me and said, "Go home, Kenny." He didn't even ask who Selena was or say anything about a merry Christmas. He has been a complete Scrooge, and I have no idea why. Just because we aren't close doesn't mean that I don't care about him being sick. It doesn't mean that I don't see any point in trying to spend time with him before he dies. And I can't think of what I possibly did to make him hate me so much.

Selena stops walking and looks up at the canopy of trees. "I can't believe I'm not seeing snow," she says, basking in the LA weather.

I stay silent next to her. I'm not in the mood to make small talk.

She closes her eyes and listens to the trees moving. I figure maybe I should do the same.

"It's quiet out here," she breathes.

I tilt my head back and keep my eyes closed, hearing nothing but the rustling leaves and the whooshing sound of passing cars. As I do this, I can feel my heart rate start to calm down.

Then suddenly, Selena puts her hand in mine. Instead of reacting right away, I keep my eyes shut and let her hold it.

"Kenneth, I have absolutely no idea what you're going through, or what you must be feeling right now. But I do know that what happened back there doesn't have to ruin our Christmas."

A lump forms in my throat. It's going to be really embarrassing if I burst out into tears right now.

Selena continues. "I think what your dad did is incredibly unfair and unreasonable. And it's horrible that he's keeping you away from him like this."

If I speak now, my voice is going to crack, and the tears are going to escape. So instead, I give her hand a gentle squeeze. She squeezes it back.

Then she continues. "For what it's worth, you are an amazing son. An amazing human *being*, really. You care about people. You deserve better."

I open my eyes to look at her, only to realize that hers are still closed, her head still tilted back at the sky.

Right here, in this moment, Selena might be one of

the most beautiful women I have ever seen. And I couldn't be more grateful that she is here with me.

Sensing me looking, Selena opens her eyes and peeks at me. Then her face twists into a smile. "I'm sure there's something else we could plan."

I already have an idea in mind. "Actually, let me make a call." I whip out my phone and go to my sister's contact info. When I call her and tell her the situation, she's more than thrilled to have me and Selena come over to her house.

"I didn't know you had a sister," Selena tells me as we get back into my car. I feel like a whole different man already than the one who had just left it.

"Yeah, two nephews, too," I tell her. I start the car and head over. On the radio, Selena fiddles with the stations until she can find one playing Christmas music. Then we both belt out Christmas carols the entire drive to my sister's house.

"UNCLE KENNY!" my youngest nephew, Noah, calls to me as Selena and I get out of the car outside of my sister's small family home.

I feel bad about not having got them gifts, so I whip out my wallet as Noah hugs my leg. At this, my other nephew, Benny, perks his head up over on the porch.

My sister, Isabell, and her husband, Josh, are standing on the porch with him waving at us. From inside their house, I can smell the fresh cinnamon rolls.

I give Noah a tight squeeze and ruffle his cute brown

head of hair, then I pull a twenty out. "Merry Christmas, kiddo," I say to him.

"Wow! I am going to buy Legos with this!" Noah tells me. I can't believe he's gotten so big already. Every time I come over, it's like they've aged a hundred years. Maybe I need to come over more often.

At least they're all happy to see me.

I hold my wallet up to Benny, who is a little bit more on the shy side. "Don't you want to see your Christmas present, too?" I ask him.

My sister gives him an encouraging little shove, and Benny steps off the porch and heads my way. Next to me, Noah is eyeing Selena. "I've never seen you before," he points out.

Selena giggles. "I'm your Uncle Kenny's friend, Selena."

Benny doesn't hug me, but he stands there with a shy smile, so it's good enough for me. I pull out another twenty and hand it over to him. Then I introduce everyone to Selena and go give my sister and brother-in-law hugs.

We all go inside the house and immediately dive into the cinnamon rolls. Even though I haven't seen my sister in months, and even though when we were texting the other day, she told me my idea to go to dad's was stupid, Isabell has always had a way of acting like everything is fine, and that no time has passed. I've always loved that about her.

And even more so, she doesn't try to push any awkward questions on Selena. She just accepts her as easily as she accepts me, regardless of not knowing whether or not she was ever going to see her again.

So, while I may not have gotten to see my dear old dad or Eliza this Christmas, and while Selena didn't get to be with her family or the people she loves, I think the two of us ended up having a pretty darn good Christmas anyway.

24

DAMASCUS

I don't want to be that person, the one who barges in on my girlfriend's Christmas when she doesn't want me there, but I just want to explain myself. I *need* to explain myself. I don't want Blair to be mad at me anymore. I don't want to be with Jennifer. The second I saw the look on Blair's face when she caught me with her at the town square yesterday, everything became clear to me. Blair is who I want to be with.

And while she might be mad at me right now, she is a girl worth fighting for.

So, hopefully she answers the door.

I walk up the icy steps to the front door of Blair's parents' house and knock a few times. It's pretty early, barely even seven, but if I know Blair, she's awake already. She lives for Christmas.

I hear shuffling coming from inside, but the person who answers the door is probably the last person I would've ever expected to see. I'm so startled that a supermodel is in Blair's parents' doorway that I gasp and fall backward off the steps and into the snow.

I don't know why I didn't put it together sooner. Giselle Cosgrove. *Blair* Cosgrove. Now that I can see Giselle up close, I see the resemblance between the two of them.

"Oh my gosh! Are you okay?" Giselle Cosgrove asks me. I stand myself up and brush the cold snow off with my bare hands.

"Yeah, sorry," I start, feeling slightly embarrassed. Then I clear my throat. "Uh, I'm here to see Blair. Is she… is she here?"

Giselle Cosgrove, the supermodel, bites her bottom lip. I partially feel like I'm dreaming. "You must be Damascus?" she says in a question-like tone.

Blair has told Giselle Cosgrove about me. A *supermodel* knows who I am. I shake my head to get rid of my overwhelmed thoughts. "Yeah, that's me."

Giselle Cosgrove only has the door open a crack, so I can't see inside their house as I slowly start back up the steps. "Um, she doesn't want to talk to you. I'm sorry."

I will tell Blair that I'm going to group therapy, even though I'm terrified of getting a similar reaction to how Jennifer had behaved, just because that's how badly I want to talk to her.

"Please, I just need like… three seconds."

Giselle Cosgrove looks apologetic. "You should go be with your family. Nice to meet you, Damascus. And… Merry Christmas."

"No, wait! Please!" I try to call out. "Blair!"

But I'm too late. Giselle Cosgrove closes the door and locks it.

Standing out here, alone and cold in the snow, I think back to last year's Christmas. With Jennifer.

She had told me she wanted it to be a normal family event for once. She said that we shouldn't do any plotting or scheming, and just have a good time. But I hated her family. I didn't want them to sit around and enjoy their Christmas. I thought they were terrible people who had horrible opinions of what the world should be like.

So, ignoring her request, I got drunk and started a debate with her father at the dinner table. It ended up getting so heated, the entire family getting involved, that Jennifer's father lunged across the table at me and grabbed me by the collar. Food flew everywhere, and everybody screamed. Jennifer was furious!

So now, it's been two Christmases in a row that I've ruined. All on my own.

I slowly walk away from Blair's house, knowing I will probably just make it worse if I try to knock again.

I can't believe it. For the first time in my entire life, I am going to be alone for Christmas.

25

BRENNAN

I don't get it. Leah had been the one who asked me to stay with her last night. She had been wasted, but she *wanted* me to stay there and take care of her. I held her hair back while she puked into her toilet. I even tried to lay her on the couch, cover her with a blanket, leave her a glass of water, and then go home, but she had specifically asked me not to. So, I didn't.

Even Henderson's is closed on Christmas, and I

don't really feel like I'm welcome at home, so I've just been wandering around outside in the freezing cold for the past hour and a half. I've pulled my phone out and gone to text Leah about a dozen times—now that I have her number—but then I stop myself. She had been furious at me this morning. I'm pretty sure I'm probably the last person she wants to hear from.

I walk to the park in my neighborhood and notice that the picnic table under the gazebo doesn't have any snow on it, so I head over and take a seat. Again, I pull my phone out and compose a text to Leah.

Then again, I erase it.

Before I can put my phone back in my pocket, it starts ringing, and my mom's number crosses the screen.

I answer with caution. "Hello?"

"Brennan, honey, where are you right now?" Mom asks me.

"I am… around," I reply.

She sighs heavily. "For the love of God, Brennan, can you please come home? It's Christmas."

My stomach twists. "I don't feel like that's a good idea," I slowly explain.

"We might be having our differences right now, but you are still family. And you should be with your *family* on Christmas. I don't want to hear any other excuses, Brennan. I'll see you soon."

She hangs up on me, so I don't even have a chance to reply.

"This cannot end well," I say under my breath as I get up from the table and put my phone away.

When I get to my parents' house, I try to let myself in quietly, hoping that maybe they won't even notice. As much as I don't enjoy the thought of spending time with them right now, I *do* enjoy the thought of being in my warm, comfortable bed. I'm not hungover or anything—I had hardly even drank last night because I was afraid I would make an ass of myself in front of Leah's family—but after standing outside in the cold for so long with a too-thin jacket, being cozied up under some covers sounds like just what I need.

Naturally, Derek is sitting on the chair in the living room that has the perfect view of me when I step inside the house. It's like he was waiting for this to happen.

His face still hasn't healed all the way, but I can't help but feel a little proud that I am the one who did that to them. He still has bruises and scabs, but to my dismay, he looks cheerier than ever.

"Merry Christmas, Little Brother," he says to me, a smile plastered on his face that is probably fake.

"Brennan!" Mom cries to me, turning around on the sofa to me. Even Dad turns and nods his head at me, too.

"Merry Christmas, everyone." I step slowly into the living room, where they're all sitting and watching *A Christmas Story*, the movie we put on every year after breakfast and presents.

Mom gets up and hugs me. It's not one of her normal hugs, but I suppose I will take what I can get. When we pull apart, I go to sit on the other recliner, on the opposite side of the fireplace from where my brother is.

"No Selena this Christmas?" I ask him.

He chuckles at me. "Spending time with her family this year," he explains. "I couldn't go with because of the games coming up."

I nod my head slowly, not believing it for a second. Maybe Selena *did* go to have Christmas with her family, but I am a hundred percent certain that she didn't want him to come with.

"Shut up and watch the movie," Dad snaps at the both of us. I shoot Derek a glare the same time he does, then we turn our focus to the screen.

LATER IN THE EVENING—WHEN we've all had our naps, and I've gotten to take a shower—I sit back in the living room on my phone, just hoping and praying that Leah will send me a text. Even a simple *Merry Christmas*.

I don't know why I'm so bothered. Who cares if she was mad at me? It's not like we are friends. It's not like we're going to make plans to hang out next week. I just happened to run into her when I was alone on Christmas Eve, and she was just a kind being who was willing to let me tag along with her family. That was that. Even if she gave me her number, that doesn't mean that I should text her.

Right?

When I look up, Derek is leaned against the stair railing, a beer in hand. "I saw you," he says.

Mom and Dad are in the kitchen, preparing for our family to come over for dinner.

"Saw me what?" I ask.

"Last night. You were with Leah. And her family."

Heavy tension hangs in the air.

Even now, seeing him standing in my parents' living room, picturing his massive hands causing small, fragile Leah any pain, makes my skin crawl.

I shrug. "It was a bar crawl. We had fun, actually."

He opens his mouth, and I know he's about to ask me what I was doing with her, but then the front door opens, and in walks the governor and his daughter.

Derek turns around. "Uncle Gerry!" he says in greeting, going to hug the man.

Governor Gerard Reiner, our uncle, hugs him back warmly. "There's my football star!"

Derek goes to hug Jennifer next, but she backs away from him with a disgusted look on her face. "Didn't you, like, hit a bunch of girls?" She isn't afraid to ask. I smile at her, and she ducks around the two to walk to the living room to see me. We hug briefly, then she pulls a flask out of her purse when her dad and Derek aren't looking. "Want some?" she asks.

I raise my eyebrows at her. My cousin has always been a little bit on the rebellious side, but she's never gotten drunk at a family gathering before.

I guess it might make it a little more fun.

"Are you even twenty-one yet?" I ask her.

"Who cares?"

I give her a lopsided smile, take the flask, and throw some back. I don't know what I expected to taste—probably something fruity—so I nearly choke on the Jack Daniels.

"Damn," I tell her as I hand the flask back.

She looks over her shoulder to make sure nobody is watching, then she throws some back herself.

"Where is Jennifer?!" I can hear my mom asking Uncle Gerry in the kitchen.

Jennifer hides the flask. "Aunt Laurie?! I've missed you!" she squeals, shooting me a wink before heading into the kitchen to greet my parents.

WHEN WE ALL sit around the formal dining table for dinner, Jennifer is plastered. The governor's daughter is plastered.

"I just don't even know how you guys are still married," she slurs to my mom and dad. "Or *you*, for the matter," she says when she turns to her dad. Then she stabs at her Christmas ham with her fork and shovels it sloppily into her mouth. "All relationships are doomed to fail at some point. So, what's the point of even getting into one?"

Uncle Gerry shakes his head. "She is still getting over that break up," he informs us.

"No, I'm not!" Jennifer argues. "*I* dumped *him*! Because all men are cheaters and liars and…" She deliberately points her fork and glares at Derek. "And wife beaters."

Uncle Gerry leaps up from the table. "That's enough, Jennifer! What's the matter with you?"

Jennifer starts giggling uncontrollably.

The governor looks at her in horror. "Are you high?"

She only laughs harder. Leave it to the governor to assume that giggling means marijuana.

Seeing the look on Derek's face as he angrily cuts his ham, I can't help but laugh a little to myself, too. I had expected the evening to be awkward and quiet. But thankfully for Jennifer, it's turning out to be quite the opposite.

26

KENNETH

I can't hide my surprise when Eliza shows up on my doorstep the next morning.

Selena and I were busy packing up our stuff and getting ready to head to the airport to go back to Quincy, and the loud knocking on my door had scared Selena nearly half to death. She even ran into the kitchen and ducked below the counter while I walked over to go answer it.

"Eliza?!" I cry out when I see her.

My stepmom is wearing an expensive fur coat and leather gloves. Her eyes are full of sadness as she stands out there in the hallway of my building.

"Oh, good," she says to me, making me step aside as she lets herself enter. "It looks like you guys are getting ready to take off. That means we must be on the same flight back to Quincy."

I was wondering why she was dressed for the cold—LA isn't exactly a place where you need a fur coat and leather gloves in the winter.

"Wait," I start, my head hurting from confusion.

Over in the kitchen, Selena slowly stands herself up and smiles brightly at Eliza.

"Were you just… hiding from me?" Eliza asks her.

Selena blushes, embarrassed. "No, no! I dropped my earring somewhere. Just… looking for it."

Eliza doesn't buy it for a second. "Were you guys expecting somebody *else* to be at the door?" she asks. "Are you two some sort of Bonnie and Clyde pair? Trying to avoid imprisonment or something"

Selena and I laugh, but it's only half-hearted on my part because I still have no idea what Eliza is doing in my apartment, and why she's saying she is coming to Quincy with us.

I step toward my stepmom and close my apartment door. "Not that I'm not thrilled to see you again—even though yesterday was kind of rough," I explain. "But… what do you mean, 'same flight to Quincy?' Why are you going there?"

Even though I can tell she's sad, she keeps an air about her that is light and casual. Probably because she is in front of a stranger and doesn't feel comfortable being her normal self. She's always putting on a show for people. I don't know how she does it.

"Your father and I got in a fight. Our Christmas was miserable."

"Okay, but that doesn't really explain why you want to come to Quincy."

Eliza has never even been to Quincy. My dad didn't meet her until after he moved out to LA.

She shrugs. "Where else would I go?" she asks me. "I want to spend time with the only other family I have —which is you and Isabell—but I want to get out of LA. So, Quincy it is."

"I'm sorry you guys are fighting," I say. "But are you sure that's a good idea? Shouldn't Dad have somebody there to take care of him?"

"There are a million people there to take care of him, I assure you. Even if I *did* stay, I wouldn't be able to do it, Kenneth. Your father told me he doesn't love me anymore. He doesn't want me around him anymore. So, now you don't have to feel like you and Isabell are the only ones."

My stomach sinks. I wish I knew why he continues to push away the people who love him, and why he's choosing to surround himself with a bunch of strangers. Who wants to live out the remainder of their life like that?

"There's no way he means that," I try to assure her.

Eliza is not normally one to cry, but I notice it when her eyes fill with tears. She tries to be quick and turn away from me, but she wasn't quick enough. "It is what it is, Kenneth. Even if he does love me, it doesn't change the fact that he doesn't want me there."

Selena and I exchange looks, and the three of us are silent for a moment.

Eventually, Eliza turns around and claps her hands together, a smile on her face. "So! You'll have to teach me how to navigate the airport. It's been a while since I've ridden on a commercial flight."

27

———

DAMASCUS

At this point, I don't even know if Blair is still my girlfriend anymore. It's New Year's Eve now, and I have still barely heard from her.

I've even tried to ask her if our relationship is over, and her reply to that had been something vague.

I don't know what I think.

That's what she had said. This was over text last night before I went to bed. I tossed and turned all night after reading it, and when I woke up this morning, I had a horrible feeling in the pit of my stomach.

When I get feelings like this, I have that urge. I want to lash out. I want to do something that will distract me. My own self-sabotaging, if you will.

Maybe Blair will get even *more* mad at me if I do something bad. Maybe she will tell me that she's done for good. But at least I'll have her attention.

And at least I will know.

I decide I'm going to go to another Warehouse party. I already know what to expect of it; it's going to look exactly like the Christmas one, only all of the red and green will be gone, and instead of ugly sweaters, everyone will be dressed up.

I don't drink beforehand this time. The reason I'm going in the first place is because I hope I see Jennifer again, and I need to be sober when I do.

The thing is, I am still reeling over how she had acted when she found out I went to group therapy. I just want to ask her what her problem is. I want to confront her about being so judgmental.

Maybe someone will see me and her fighting, and they will tell Blair about it. Then Blair will know that Jennifer doesn't mean anything to me.

Because she doesn't. I swear.

I put on the only formal clothes I have—a black button-up shirt, black slacks, and my black and white sneakers. Then I look in the mirror and think about doing something about my messy hair, but I don't.

It's not like Blair will be there for me to try and impress.

I drive to The Warehouse in my truck and park, then I hop out and head inside.

The music in here is so loud that I can feel it vibrating in my chest, and there's even more people here than before, too. It almost looks like all of Quincy has decided to show up.

It's already a little after eleven, and I know I don't have much time until midnight. I also know that I can't be next to Jennifer when the countdown happens. She is not the way I want to start off my new year—I want to use these last fifty-one minutes to make sure she's not in my new year at *all*.

I go to the dance floor first, since that's where I had luck last time, but Jennifer is nowhere to be found. I walk over to the bar, and Jennifer isn't there, either. I turn and head up the old metal steps to the second level, but on the third step, I look up and see my girlfriend heading down them.

We both freeze at the same time, five steps between us. She looks beautiful. Her dress is black and covered in sequins, and it reminds me a little bit of those twenties flapper dresses. Her hair is curled in sexy waves, and her eye makeup is dark and desirable. I've never even seen her dressed like this before.

"Damascus!" she gasps. The sound of her saying my name makes my heart leap.

"Blair?" I wonder if maybe my eyes are deceiving me. "What are you doing here?"

"I am here for the New Year's Eve party."

"Well, duh, but…" I trail off. Blair normally isn't the type to come to a party like this. She would rather spend

New Year's Eve cozied up on the couch, watching the ball drop and playing board games.

But seeing her standing before me, dressed the way she is, I wonder if maybe I don't know Blair as much as I thought I did.

"I'm kidding," she says. "My sister dragged me here. She used to come to these all the time when she was in high school. She pretty much *insisted* on doing my hair and makeup, too, by the way."

Relief floods me. And the casualness of her tone makes me feel like she actually wants to talk to me. Hopefully, I'm not crazy.

"You look incredible," I tell her.

She raises her eyebrows at me. "*That's* what you want to say?"

"Yes?"

"Nothing about the fact that Giselle Cosgrove is my older sister?"

"Why would I want to stand here and talk about your sister?" I ask. "Especially when I don't know how long it's going to be before you stop talking to me again."

Somebody comes down the stairs behind Blair, so the two of us get out of the way and walk over by the bar.

When I turn to her to continue, she throws her arms around me in a hug. I squeeze her back, never wanting to let go.

Her eyes are glistening when she steps back. "What were you doing with her?"

I can barely hear her over the music, but leaping at

the chance, I am quick to explain everything that happened between Jennifer and me. I even consider telling Blair about the fact that I had been outside my support group, but at the last second, something in my head stops me.

When I'm finished explaining and apologizing, Blair nods in acceptance of my apology and fiddles with the buttons on my shirt. "I'm sorry for not letting you explain yourself sooner. I just… I know how much you loved her, and part of me wonders if you would take her back if she asked you to."

I vigorously shake my head. "Not a chance, Blair. I mean it."

She does that thing she does. She chews on her bottom lip and avoids my gaze.

"What is it?" I ask.

"If we're going to do this, Jennifer has to stay out of the picture. And whoever that other girl you were with is, has to, too."

I laugh at her. "That was Leah. You don't have to worry about her. She's like a big sister to me." Then I pull her in for another hug and kiss the top of her head. I know Blair isn't the person I meant to find here, but for once, I am proud of myself for making the right decision.

It led me back to her.

28

———

KENNETH

"So, we're going to The Warehouse party?" Selena asks me.

"Only if you're sure you want to," I say. "There will be so many people there that I doubt anyone will even realize we went together."

Selena crosses her arms, all dolled up in a champagne-colored tight, metallic dress. She's going to freeze her butt off, but she told me her outfit is worth it.

"I don't care about being seen with you anymore,"

she admits, and as proud as I am of her taking a step in the right direction, I think she's forgetting something.

"Oh, that's… great. However, it's sort of *me* who can't be seen with *you*."

She winces, but still looks as beautiful as ever.

After having such an amazing Christmas with her, and a fun few days afterward, I have finally admitted to myself that I have feelings for her. I've had them for a while, even.

"Well, I will be on my best behavior," Selena says to me. Then she gives me an excited little shimmy and dashes out of the rental house to my Subaru.

I had invited Eliza to come with us, too, but she told me she preferred to meet some of her old friends and do something quieter. I don't know which old friends she could possibly have in Quincy, but I figure they're people that Dad introduced her to.

About an hour and a half into The Warehouse party, Steve has me drunk. Shot after shot of tequila, he won't stop them coming. And landing Giselle Cosgrove as his girlfriend has turned him into an entirely different person. He no longer wants to talk about himself, and instead, he keeps asking me about *my* life while Giselle is wandering through The Warehouse, mingling with her old high school friends.

I've just spent the last ten minutes going over how stressed out I am about getting a story on Derek.

Steve slaps my shoulder. "You know, I could probably get you a job anywhere. Who cares if you lose this one?"

I groan and put my elbows on the bar top. "Yeah, but I am practically *living* with the woman who could give me the best exclusive out there. And she won't let me!" I run my hands through my hair and mess it up, too drunk to care.

"Do you really need her permission?" Steve asks.

"Yeah," I sulk. Then I let out an outrageous sigh and turn to face him. "Because I have feelings for her now, *somehow*. So, I can't do anything to hurt her."

Steve raises his eyebrows at me. "Holy shit."

I'm not usually one to fall for chicks. It's not that I don't want to settle; it's just that none of them have been worth it. None of them have been Selena.

"I need another," I hear myself saying. Then I wave over one of the bartenders, and Steve gets us two more shots.

"You are in love with Derek Heed's wife?" he continues.

I nod my head miserably. "No—I don't *love* her. I just… I have *feelings* for her. I have feelings for her, and she won't leave *him*. Why the hell won't she leave him?"

The bartender hands us our shots, and when I throw mine back this time, I don't even taste it anymore.

I'm going to regret this.

"Well, heads up," Steve says, "she's coming behind you."

I turn around and shoot the beautiful Selena a grin. We had come into the party at separate times, so anyone watching us talk to each other now will think it's just a friendly *hello*.

Selena takes one look at the eight shot glasses sitting in between Steve and me, and she widens her eyes. "Whoa, have you two been here all night?"

Steve steps toward Selena and places a hand on her shoulder. "Kenneth has a lot of built-up stress, you know? He needs to let it out more often."

I roll my eyes and push him away from her. She doesn't like to be touched by strangers. Even drunk, I can remember that.

Steve laughs as Selena shoots me an appreciative look.

"What has you so stressed out?" she asks me.

"Well, his boss is going to fire him, for one," Steve answers for me.

I whirl my head to him angrily. That was not something I wanted her to know.

Selena tries to get my attention. "Wait. *Fired?*" She grabs my shoulder and turns me back to her. "What is he talking about, Kenny?"

"I'll be going now," Steve says, slapping me on the back and walking off into the crowd.

I look at Selena. Right now, there are two of her.

"Kenneth," she repeats.

"Well, yeah, you know," I say. "Because you won't let me write the piece on Derek. You don't want to come forward and admit that the anonymous posts are from us." I turn and pick up one of the shot glasses, convinced that there's still liquid inside of it. I frown when I notice that it's empty.

"You never mentioned to me that you were going to lose your *job* if you didn't," she says, taking the shot glass out of my hand and setting it back down on the counter. I know she wants me to look at her, but I just can't.

"I don't want you to feel pressured," I explain. "I care about you, you know? And you're not ready, so there was no point in telling you."

"I… but, that is… *wow*." Selena apparently can't find the words to say.

I suck in a breath. "When *will* you be ready?"

"What?"

"Derek. When will you be ready to leave Derek?" Even saying his name makes the anger instant inside of me.

"I… Kenneth, are you drunk?"

"Stop deflecting."

"You know it's not that simple."

"No. You know that it *is*. But you still won't do it."

"Why does it matter to you so much?"

"Why does it…?" I slam a fist on the counter. "Are you kidding me, Selena?!"

She jumps back in fright.

I step away from the counter and run a hand over my face. "Shit, Selena, I'm sorry."

What the hell is the matter with me?

Selena doesn't say anything back, but the way she stares at me nearly breaks my heart.

Then just like that, she disappears.

29

GISELLE

’m standing at the bar inside The Warehouse with Kenneth and Steve when I hear the news.

"By the way, you know my stepmom, right?" Kenneth asks Steve, capturing my attention.

Steve nods at him. The two haven't stopped drinking since we got here.

"She's here right now. Came on the flight back home with us," Kenneth says.

"Wait, here in *town*?" I ask, side-glancing at Steve.

Kenneth looks at me and nods. "You know her, too?"

"Oh, she *knows* her, that's for sure," Steve says. I bug my eyes out at him, and he chuckles. "Giselle models for her."

I stop listening. Eliza is in Quincy. Why would she come here? This isn't her hometown. She's never even been outside of LA.

<hr>

IT'S PRETTY easy for me to escape The Warehouse unseen. Thank God that Steve has his friend there to keep him entertained.

The moment I leave, I take off in my parents' car. They let me borrow it for the evening since I'm supposed to be the designated driver for Blair.

I'm not exactly sure where Eliza could be right now, but Quincy is a small town. And seeing how Eliza has relatively expensive taste, the number of hotel options that would be suitable for her are extremely limited.

Not really knowing if I'm doing the right thing, I drive to the Renegade Hotel, Quincy's version of a Four Seasons. Then I park my parents' car and dash inside the lobby.

I don't see Eliza anywhere, but why was I expecting to?

I am being crazy, I tell myself as I walk over to one of the plush armchairs and take a seat.

If Eliza had meant to see me, she would have called me to let me know.

I pull my phone out of my small clutch to check for notifications, just in case I somehow missed a message from her. My phone screen remains blank. And the time reads nearly midnight. It's almost New Years, and I am about to ring it in alone in a hotel lobby.

When I look up, I see that even the hotel staff is gathering around behind the reception desk with champagne flutes full of probably cider.

I can't believe what a huge loser I'm being. *If anyone on Instagram could see me now*, I joke to myself.

I watch my phone screen, and the time reads two minutes before midnight.

I sigh and stand up. I don't know if being in the hotel lobby or in my parents' car is a worse way to ring in the new year, but at least if I go to the car, no one will see me cry.

I just want to see Eliza again so badly that it hurts.

"Giselle?"

I snap my head up, and there Eliza is, walking in through the hotel lobby doors. She has on a giant, white fur coat, a glossy white beret, and black leather gloves. Her cheeks are rosy, and the tip of her nose is red from the cold.

She looks absolutely breathtaking.

"Oh my gosh," I breathe.

Eliza approaches me. Thankfully, she is smiling. "What on earth are you doing here?"

"I was looking for you."

"Me? How did you even know…?"

"Steve isn't really my boyfriend," I admit without thinking. I just can't hold it in anymore. I don't want to start the new year with lies.

She purses her lips and draws her eyebrows together. "What do you mean?"

"Eliza, I have to tell you the truth." My heart is pounding, and my throat feels dry.

She stands there and waits for me.

"Steve saw us in the stairwell that day," I admit. "He watched us kiss. And he took a photograph of it. Ever since that day, he's been blackmailing me."

It's difficult for me to gauge her expression. "Oh…"

I take both of her hands. "It has nothing to do with you—Steve loves you. This is all *my* fault. He has feelings for me, and I didn't return them, so this was his way of getting back at me. I'm so sorry."

She looks deep into my eyes. "So, you're not with him?" she asks.

"It's all fake. I don't have feelings for him, Eliza." I step closer to her, her hands still in mine. "It's impossible for me to have feelings for him, actually."

Eliza can tell where I'm going with this. She gives me a knowing look. "Giselle…," she warns.

"What, Eliza?" I ask. "All I know is that I can't stop thinking about you."

Behind the reception desk, the hotel staff begins counting down from ten.

Eliza's mouth keeps opening and closing, a total loss for words.

"And you can try to deny it all you want, Eliza

Leon," I continue, "but I know you have feelings for me, too. You wouldn't be here, otherwise."

She gives me a sly smile and steps closer to me. "You're right."

The hotel staff counts down to one, then they all yell, "Happy New Year!"

At the same time, Eliza and I tilt our heads toward each other, and then finally, I get to kiss her again.

30

KENNETH

I am going to blame Steve for getting me so belligerently wasted last night. It was so bad that I didn't even remember coming home last night.

But when I wake up this morning, my head pounding and my stomach rolling. I manage to get out of bed and leave my bedroom to go see if Selena is awake yet. I am assuming she is because it is already past noon.

The second I step into the hallway, I notice that her

bedroom door is closed. Feeling dizzy and slightly like I might still be drunk, I step carefully toward the kitchen.

Selena isn't here.

Is she still asleep?

"Selena?"

I'm about to go peek my head into her room, but then a piece of paper on the counter stops me. It's a note:

I'm going to go stay with my parents for a while. Thank you for everything you've done.

Selena

I read the note over a hundred times. I know Selena and I got in a bit of an argument last night—in fact, it's one of the last things I remember about my New Year's Eve. But before that ever happened, Selena had told me she didn't want to see her parents. She said they were overbearing and too far away, and that Derek would find her there in an instant. Did I really piss her off so badly that she would rather risk being found by him than stay here for one more second with me?

31

BRENNAN

My Christmas had been so eventful that I decided a low-key New Year's Eve was the only way I wanted to spend the holiday. Not only had Jennifer been drunk and hysterical on Christmas, but Derek had also confessed to Mom and Dad late at night after the governor and Jennifer had left, that Selena had left him. That she couldn't handle the stress and the pressure of being with him when he was going through all these accusations.

Then my brother swore to my parents that he never laid a hand on her, and he even broke down into tears. My naïve, Derek-loving parents consoled him and told him how everything was going to be just fine.

I sat on the staircase during this, far enough up on the steps where they couldn't see me from the living room. As I listen to Derek speak, I couldn't help but tear up myself. Not because I felt bad for my brother—the opposite, actually. I felt bad for Selena. For how I had spent all these past years treating her.

Once, a long time ago, back when Selena and Derek first got engaged, Selena had confronted me about something. She had told me that she and Derek got into a fight over the guestlist for the wedding, and that he had gotten "violent" and "aggressive" with her.

You see, back then, I was blinded by Derek, just like everybody else is now. I thought there was no way Derek would ever be that kind of man. Selena had seemed to only start being interested in him when he started growing in popularity. I thought my older brother was this amazing person, and that Selena was an influencer wannabe who was lying to me for attention. I figured she was saying what she could to blackmail Derek into staying with her because she was worried that Derek was going to leave her for somebody more famous.

I have been wanting to find Selena and apologize to her for a while now. I just don't even know if I can find the right words to say. I don't know how I would do it. I owe her so much. She had tried to tell me that she was in trouble, and I did *nothing* to help. Every time I think about the night she made her confession to me, I want to punch something. That might've been her *one* cry for help, and the fact that I shut her down so fast could have been why she kept quiet about it ever since. I probably convinced her that nobody would ever be on her side about this.

I decide to keep my shop open and run it all by myself on New Year's Day. Then when I get home in the evening, I find Mom and Dad in the kitchen, looking happier than they have been in a while.

I walk over to the fridge and open it up to grab some leftovers. The entire time I move around the kitchen, I can feel their eyes on me.

"What's up?" I ask them after popping a Tupperware full of sausages and beans into the microwave.

"Your dad and I thought you should know," Mom begins, "Selena came home early this morning. Back to Derek. She is going to stay by his side through the rest of this and show her support."

Great, now I'm not hungry anymore. And those beans and sausages had been sounding so good all day while I was at work.

I nod my head. "And you two believe him?"

"We raised him, Brennan." Dad crosses his arms. "And we raised a good man. I don't know why you are so quick to believe everyone else's lies, but Derek isn't doing what they are all saying."

"Just because you raised him to be better, doesn't mean he didn't turn out badly anyway," I try to explain. "Who he turned out to be, it's not your fault. You couldn't have controlled the hatred and anger issues he carries around inside."

Dad looks angry. "Brennan, if you can't support your family during a time like this, then I don't think you are going to be welcome in this house for much longer."

The microwave beeps, but nobody moves to open it. "You know what? You're right," I say. "I'll start shopping around today. Because if I stay here in this house with you, it's only going to make me look like I *do* support him. That I'm on his side about all of this. But I'm not. That's why I beat the shit out of him. Because he deserved it."

I take my keys off of the hook by the door and leave, slamming it shut behind me.

Looks like I'm having fast food for dinner.

32

DAMASCUS

"Shawn has decided he's going to be joining our session over video call," Leah informs our support group the day after New Year's Day.

I smile as she gets her projector screen set up so that she can call him in.

The rest of the class talks and murmurs in excitement about getting to hear from him, too. A lot of them are only excited because Shawn is a famous artist, but I am excited because I care about him and enjoy speaking with him. Now that Blair and I have stopped fighting, I don't feel so lousy and grumpy, and I'm doing what I can to stay that way. I think Shawn needs to do this, too.

When Shawn is finally on the screen, everyone waves at him.

Leah has rearranged the circle of chairs today in more of an oval shape so that Shawn's screen can be a part of it.

"Can you see us all okay?" Leah asks him. Shawn, looking tired and slightly pale, nods.

Leah sits in her chair. "Great," she says. "Let's get started then. How has everybody been feeling? Especially with the holiday season?"

To everyone's astonishment, Shawn is the first one to speak. He usually only said anything if he was called on. "I don't know how much time I have on here today," he explained to the class, "so I better get this out. Especially before I change my mind."

"Alright, Shawn. I love it," Leah says. "How are you? How was your Christmas and New Year?"

It sucks to see and hear Shawn as progressed into his ALS as he is. Every time I talk to him, he's worse.

Shawn hangs his head, and the lump that forms in my throat is instant. "It was miserable. I have been a fool." I've never seen him this way. "I have pushed everyone away. Everyone. Not even Eliza is here with me now. I thought I was doing the right thing. I thought it would be better if they could remember me in more of a healthier light. Nobody wants to be seen like this. Nobody wants to be waited on every second of every day. Especially not when I'm the one who used to do all of the waiting. I was supposed to take care of Eliza. Not the other way around. I was supposed to take care of my kids. My grandkids. Not the other way around—at least not for much, *much* longer than this."

He paused for a moment before continuing. "I was proud and bitter. And after having a miserable Christmas and spending New Year with only the company of my medical team and my butler, all I want is to go back in time. I just want to do it all over. Even all the bullshit of my disease. I spent too much time hating myself and wanting to keep my sense of pride. Now my time is almost up. And I'll never be able to make up for the time I've wasted."

There is not a dry eye in the room. Even when I look at Leah, I can tell that she is trying her best to remain composed.

She clears her throat. "Well… that, uh, that seems tough."

He slowly nods his head. His eyes are bloodshot, and his bottom lip is quivering.

"So then, Shawn, you know what you have to do, right?" I ask.

"Is that you speaking, Damascus?" Shawn asks. "What do I have to do?"

I wipe my eyes and sit up straighter. "You have to stop wasting any more of the time you still have. Not a single second of it."

33

KENNETH

I go to the game today because I need to try and gauge Derek's behavior. The moment I notice that he is being cockier and smiling more than normal, I am worried. What if Selena's parents couldn't be trusted? What if the second she arrived at their house, they phoned Derek to let him know? Derek was able to convince his entire family that he's a good person. What if he had been able to fool Selena's family as well?

It's cold and cloudy out, the snow coming down on and off every couple of minutes. With numb fingers because I forgot my gloves, I pull out my phone and try Selena's cell. Again, she doesn't answer. I haven't even been able to bring myself to go back and count how many times I've tried. It's too embarrassing. But all I want to do is apologize to her. I can't stand the thought of her hating me, and I can't stand not knowing if she is okay.

"Um, are you Kenneth?"

I turn around to a woman whose skin is almost as white as the snow falling from the sky. Her dark brown hair is pin-straight around her face, and she's bundled up in warm winter clothes.

"Yes, I am." I stick out my hand, and she gives it a quick shake. She looks familiar, but I'm just not entirely sure why.

"I'm Leah," she starts. "You may not remember me because I was quite a few years behind you in school, but I think we've talked a few times growing up. At the park and stuff."

It hits me. We lived in neighborhoods across the way from each other and would frequent the same park that was in her neighborhood because it had the better field to play sports on. Sometimes Leah joined in on our games of tag.

"Leah, yeah! I do remember you, actually. Wow. How are you?" A lot of people around Quincy have recognized me since I've been back, but not many of them have tried to make conversation. Especially not ones who hardly know me. I look down and notice that she doesn't have a ring on her finger. Vaguely, I wonder if she's here to hit on me.

Her smile turns to a grimace at my question. "Well, to be honest, normally I wouldn't be caught dead at a place like this," she informs me. "But it's a long story."

"I see."

I look over at the game just as Derek is scoring a touchdown. The crowd goes wild, and Derek does a dance. Thankfully, I do hear a few boos in the stands, too.

"I noticed you over here, and thought I would come talk to you about something," she says. Blush is creeping into her cheeks as she avoids my eyes.

"Really? About what?"

"Well, I can't say much because I signed an NDA." She hugs herself. "But I just think you should know. Your father, Shawn? He really loves you."

At the mention of an NDA, I had been expecting this conversation to be about Derek. About how she had been paid to keep quiet about something. Her mentioning my father is the last thing I would have thought.

I raise an eyebrow. "How do you know my father?"

"I can't really say, but did you know that I run a couple of support groups at the town center?" She looks at me with big eyes as she nods her head slowly, trying to get me to understand. I think I do. My dad must have been in one of her groups. Or maybe Eliza went to one when she was here recently.

I give her a smile, even though I don't feel happy about her statement. "Oh. Um, well, thank you for letting me know, Leah. Uh, yeah… It would be nice to hear *him* say that, however." Maybe she will pass along the message.

She nods her head. "He will. Just hang in there."

I scratch my chin, not knowing how to reply. Then I think maybe the conversation is over, and she's going to go back to wherever she was sitting, but she doesn't move.

"And I am…" She trails off and sucks in a breath. I'm not at all expecting the next things that come out of her mouth. "Well, I guess I'm just gonna come right out and say it. I knew you were here. It's why I came. Not just to tell you about your dad. But I was also wondering if you would be willing to take a statement from me. Not anonymously."

I am so confused. Because she can't possibly mean what it is I think she means. What it is I desperately want her to be meaning. "A statement?"

She looks confused, too. But when she clarifies, goosebumps of relief flood across my entire body. "I don't know how any of this works, but I heard you need a story on Derek Heed. And I want to give you one."

34

———

GISELLE

Am I a horrible human being? Should I even be in this house right now, right beside Shawn after I spent New Year's Eve alone in Eliza's hotel room with her? Shawn is dying! And here I am, at their beachfront mansion because Eliza asked me to, acting like I don't care. I do care, but Eliza told me she needed me. She had to go home and face her husband eventually, and she wanted me by her side. We had both agreed to keep what happened between us a secret.

When we got back from Quincy, I had work to do, photoshoots to attend, along with making appearances with Steve so that the public thinks we are still together. Then after all of that was done, I told Eliza I was free, and she begged me to come over.

I'm not exactly sure why I'm here, because Eliza is hard at work preparing for an oncoming fashion show—she's running around her mansion like a maniac and keeps leaving me alone with Shawn.

"I'm guessing you've been mad at me, too," Shawn says to me in the living room. He is sitting on his recliner, and I am on the sofa.

"What do you mean?" I ask, my hands on my knees and my posture still.

"Well, I'm sure Liza told you about Christmas."

"She did. I'm the one who convinced her that you didn't mean what you said." He had told Eliza he wanted a divorce. I knew it wasn't true. He was being irrational.

Shawn nods his head. "I'm glad she had you there in Quincy to comfort her," he says. Then the look he gives me is so intense that my heart begins hammering, and my stomach feels like it might fly out of my butt.

Does he know?

I don't think Eliza would have told him what happened between us in my hometown, but that doesn't mean that Shawn couldn't have deduced the truth on his own.

"Well, you're welcome," I say. This feels all wrong. Normally, I would be joking around with him and calling him Shawnie. Now I don't know how to act.

Maybe I should stop considering trying to break into the acting industry because, clearly, I am no good. It's a wonder that my act with Steve is working at all. Steve could ruin me. He could ruin Eliza. We both know it.

And I'm terrified that no matter what lies I spew, no matter how I treat him and follow along with his black-mailing plot, he still might tell the world the truth.

"I'm welcome?" Shawn asks.

"I'm sorry, I'm sorry! I'll be right down!" Eliza yells from somewhere upstairs.

I look at Shawn. "Yeah. Because she was hysterical. You hurt her, and she was close to believing that you were being truthful. You could have lost her forever, Shawn. Is that what you want?"

I know what I'm doing is so *wrong*.

I already struggle to understand what Shawn is saying when he's trying to speak normally, so I can barely make out a word as he stutters nervously. The only thing I get is, "No."

The next thing I tell him is because I know it's true. It doesn't matter what I want. Love isn't about that. It's about what the people you love need. "Eliza loves you. She's not still with you because she has to be. You clearly have a lot of other people who can take care of you. She is still with you because she wants to be." Then I stand up. I can't stand being alone with him right now. "I'm going to go see if she needs help."

My heart is aching. It feels as if it's tearing. Tearing because of my own words. Because of the truth of it all.

Shawn doesn't do anything except stare at me as I leave the room.

He and Eliza are supposed to be together. And as much as I want to be with her, all I am doing in the long run is causing more harm than good to everyone around me.

What I've done is wrong. Being here now is wrong. I need to do better.

What the hell is the matter with me?

35

———

BRENNAN

I can't consciously be okay about Selena being with my horrid older brother. Besides, it's about time I finally apologize.

So, when one of Derek's important football games is going on at the stadium, I get in my car—after making sure my employees will be okay at the shop without me for a bit—then I head to Derek and Selena's gated house once more.

This time, when I pull up to the entrance, I am a

little more cautious to see if there are any lookers nearby, but since Derek is at the game, no one is around. I park the car in the circular driveway and get out, my stomach twisting with nervousness. When I walk up the porch steps and knock on the iron door, I mutter my rehearsed speech.

Slowly, the door creaks open. Selena is wearing long sleeves, long pants, and long socks. She looks tired, and as if she's trying to cover it up with makeup.

"Brennan?" she asks. "What are you doing here?"

I begin choking. Suddenly, I don't remember a single thing I had planned to say to her. "Uh… Derek—I just —I talked to Leah. You don't know who she is. But—" I pause for a moment. *Get it together!*

Her eyebrows clash together understandably. I'm not making a word of sense. "Derek isn't here," she points out.

"Yeah, I know that." I shake my head repeatedly. "Selena, I am so sorry. I should've believed you when you tried to warn me about him way back when."

Now it's Selena's turn to forget how to speak. "Oh," she manages.

"Nothing I can tell you will ever make up for it. I just hope you know that I am on your side. Derek's ex-girlfriend, her name is Leah. I've been talking to her a lot, and she's told me a bit about what he's done." I grimace at the mention of Leah's name because it reminds me of Christmas morning. Since then, we haven't spoken.

"I know who Leah is."

"Oh?" This is news to me.

She nods. "We talk almost every day. On Instagram. She's really good at helping me feel better."

"She never mentioned that to me. But it makes sense; she's good with people. She runs some support groups."

"Yeah, I know."

We stare at each other for a beat. "Did you… did you make the anonymous post?" I finally ask.

"This isn't the best place to talk about that." Then she motions in front of her chest upwards and mouths the word "cameras" to me.

I nod my head. "You really shouldn't be here. Isn't there anywhere else you could stay?"

"I want to be here." Her eyes say the exact opposite. She is trapped here. Imprisoned.

"What can I do?" I ask, bringing my voice down to a whisper so maybe the cameras won't pick it up. "Please, just tell me."

"So, have you talked to Leah lately?" she asks, abruptly changing the subject.

"No. She's mad at me."

"Do you know why?"

I shake my head. "Why? Did she say something to you?"

"Leah was terrified when she found you in her house on Christmas. She said she was scared because she blacked out and doesn't remember anything that happened the night before. She doesn't know if you took advantage of her."

My eyes widen in horror. "I didn't! I swear. I—she asked me to take care of her. I would never…" I feel horrible. Not to mention angry. It's Derek's fault that she thinks like this. I'm not like him, but I don't know if she will ever fully believe that.

If anyone will ever fully believe that.

"You are a good guy, Brennan," Selena says. "You do a lot for the people you care about, even if you're caring about the wrong ones. I understand why you ignored me when I tried to talk to you before. You barely even knew me."

I'm grateful for her saying it, but I'm confused about why she changed the subject again.

She continues. "So, I know that you didn't do anything with Leah. I know that you wouldn't, and I told her that. I told her to trust her gut, which was telling her that you wouldn't ever hurt her. She has never had a guy at her house before—did you know that?"

Now it makes even more sense as to why she freaked out.

"I definitely didn't. I would've never gone inside if I did. I was honestly just trying to help her." Christmas Eve had been the most fun I've had in a while, and it really sucks that Leah isn't speaking to me at all now.

I can hear a TV on in the background inside the house. Selena turns her head to look at it for a moment. Then she leaves the door open. "You can come in."

I follow her inside, feeling weird about how Derek now has cameras everywhere. We walk over to the TV in her living room. Derek's game is on.

"They… they *lost*." Selena stands there in a daze.

"Wow." It's the only thing I can manage to say

because fear and worry have taken over my ability to do anything else.

This was their last chance. Now Derek's football season is officially over. And he's not going to be happy about it. And with him not being happy…

Who knows what he will do next?

The End

CHRISTMAS CONFESSIONS

BOOK TWO OF THE MISSED CONNECTIONS TRILOGY

KATHRYN REIGN